# WITH A **Zero** AT ITS *heart*

## ALSO BY CHARLES LAMBERT

*Little Monsters*
*Any Human Face*
*The Scent of Cinnamon*
*The View from the Tower*
*The Slave House*

WITH A *Zero* AT ITS *heart*

## CHARLES LAMBERT

The Friday Project
An imprint of HarperCollins*Publishers*
77–85 Fulham Palace Road
Hammersmith, London W6 8JB
www.harpercollins.co.uk

First published by The Friday Project in 2014

1

A catalogue record for this book
is available from the British Library

ISBN 978-0-00-754551-3

Typeset in Hoefler Text by Palimpsest Book Production Limited,
Falkirk, Stirlingshire
Printed and bound in Great Britain by Clays Ltd, St Ives plc

This novel is entirely a work of fiction.

**MIX**
Paper from
responsible sources
FSC www.fsc.org
**FSC™ C007454**

FSC™ is a non-profit international organisation established to
promote the responsible management of the world's forests.
Products carrying the FSC label are independently certified to
assure consumers that they come from forests that are managed
to meet the social, economic and ecological needs of present
and future generations, and other controlled sources.

Find out more about HarperCollins and the environment at
www.harpercollins.co.uk/green

For my mother, Olive Kate Florrie Lambert
(née Preece)
1916–2011

and my father, Vincent Lambert
1905–2006

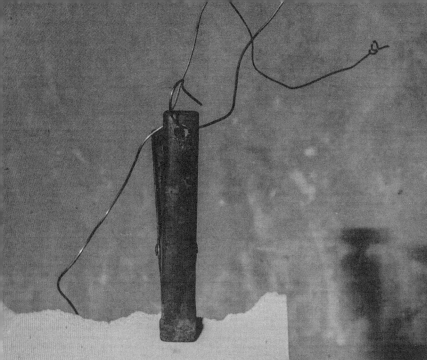

# OBJECTS

OR

*ghost balloons*

*1*  He has never seen a ship inside a bottle but the day he discovers their existence he knows that he wants one more than anything in the world. He is seven years old. He imagines men no bigger than his fingertip working at the building of the ship, singing as they nail long boards to the hull and sew the rigid sailcloth panels for the mast, tall and straight as a tree, and coat the ship with burning tar to make sure it never sinks. He watches them gather on the deck. There is a bird above their heads. He imagines he is on a ship and there is glass all around him, as far as the eye can see.

*2*  He comes across the pendant in his great-aunt's drawer. It is heavy, warm in his hand, the size of a just-fledged bird. At the heart of the pendant is the skeletal form of some insect, some winged insect, more than an inch long, longer than any insect he has ever seen, its flesh eaten out and engulfed by the same warm yellow that surrounds it. It is hollowed and sustained, its wings barely furled, it floats in this substance for which he has no name, which could be plastic but isn't. There is a loop for a chain at the top, but he will never wear it. It is amber. The insect has been trapped inside for a million years.

*3*  His father buys him a bicycle, but it is the wrong sort. The bicycle he wants has swept-down racing handlebars and no mudguards and is green and white. This one has small wheels and can fold into two. It is the colour of bottled damsons. He pushes his new bicycle into the road and rides away as hard and fast as he can, but it is not fast enough; it will never be fast enough to escape the shame of the thing that bears him. His eyes are blinded by tears. When he skids and scrapes the skin from his arms he is glad. He shows his father the blood. This is your blood, he thinks but dare not say.

*4*  He finds an owl pellet in the barn beside his house. It is round, the weight of a dove's egg, and roughly made, as though pressed from earth or some other substance he can't identify. He does what he's read in his book, soaking and prising it apart. Some of it crumbles and is thrown away, but he's left in the end with a tangle of tiny bones, as fine as rain and puzzling, like a jigsaw without its box. One by one, he lays the bones out on his table until he finds at their heart a hollow skull, a jewel. That night he sees an owl swoop from the bare eye of the barn towards his bedroom window.

5  His favourite aunt gives him a typewriter. The first thing he writes is a story about people who gather in a room above a shop to invoke the devil. When they hear the clatter of cloven hooves on the stairs the story ends, but the typewriter continues to tap out words, and then paragraphs, and then pages until the floor is covered. He picks them up and places them in a box as fast as they come, and then a second box, and then a third. There is no end to it. I am nothing more than a channel, he whispers to himself, and the typewriter pauses for a moment and then, on a new sheet, types the word Possession.

6  He's looking for Christmas presents in an antique shop behind the station when he sees a small, black lacquered box with a hinged lid. On the lid is a row of Chinamen. Their robes are exquisitely traced in gold, their wise heads tiny ovals of ivory, inset, like split peas bleached to bone. They seem to be waiting to be received like supplicants before an invisible benefactor, some mandarin perhaps. Many years later, the box survives a fire, but the shine of its lacquer is destroyed and the fine gold lines that delineate the robes of the men are seared away. What's left is the row of heads, like ghost balloons, tethered down by invisible cords to the general darkness.

7 He reads his work at an international poetry festival. The local paper calls him a small, bearded man with one earring, which is two parts false and two parts true. At the party that evening, horribly drunk, coked-up, he pretends to adore the work of a Scottish poet, whose shallow musings he despises, and ignores the two poets he most admires out of shyness and misplaced pride. These poets both die soon after, the first beneath a passing car, the second alone, choked by her own vomit. He feels accountable for their deaths. He takes the reading fee he has been given and uses it to buy a Bullworker – a contraption of wires and steel that will make him invincible.

8 Before leaving the country he buys himself a single-lens reflex camera. It is more than he can afford, but how else will they believe him? Without the lens his eye is drawn by what moves, by skin and sinew and eyes and mouths, by the shifting of an arm against a table or the way one shoulder lifts without the other, but he's too inhibited to photograph what he sees. He's scared it might answer him back. Through his lens, what he sees is the perfect empty symmetry of doors and windows, and the way light catches the concrete of a bollard a boy has been sitting on moments before, the light still there, the warmth refusing to be held.

9   They live in a rented house with a billiards room, a spiral staircase and a ghost. The local laundrette is filled with drunken Irish poets. It is cold, and getting colder daily. When they're forced to move, traipsing knee-deep in snow through the back streets of London, they take a single trophy with them, a Chinese duck with a pewter body, and brass wings and beak. The duck splits into two across the middle; they use it to keep dope, papers, all they need to hold the misery of their failure at bay. It is their stash duck and they love it. Everything else from that time has gone, everything except the ghost. The ghost is alive inside the duck.

10  His father keeps his ties in a flat wooden box. Each tie is tightly rolled, with the wide end at its heart. There are ties of all widths, all styles. His father throws nothing away and will never leave the house without a tie. The ties are held in place by a wooden grille, placed over them before the lid is closed. His father dies and he finds himself with the box of ties, many of them gifts he has bought at airports or hurriedly in shops he would normally avoid. He opens the box and rolls the ties open across his bed, their silk and wool a reproach to him as they wait to be taken up and worn.

CLOTHES

2

OR

*unripe strawberries*

*1* His first pair of long trousers are rust-coloured jeans his mother buys him from a catalogue. He's ten years old, his legs are sweaty. He rolls the jeans up at the bottom, cowboy-style, and wears them with a brand-new green pullover from the same catalogue, then goes to play with his friend next door. He's tense, excited. He feels that he has finally grown up. His friend's mother opens the door to him, before calling up the stairs to tell her daughter he's here. I hope you aren't planning on doing anything dirty, she shouts, flicking ash into her free hand. Your little friend looks ready to muck out stables. He blushes. He hates the woman with all his heart.

*2* He wants a velvet frock coat like the ones worn by The Kinks. He's seen them in a shop down the road from Beatties, called Loo Bloom's. He hadn't noticed it before, but now he stands outside the window and stares at the mannequins for hours at a time. His favourite coat is burgundy crushed velvet, with metal buttons that go from the collar to the waist. He has no trousers he could wear it with, but that doesn't matter, not yet. It will soon be Christmas. His mother hasn't said no, which gives him hope. Christmas morning he unwraps a double-breasted jacket in dark green corduroy, which he hangs in his wardrobe that evening and will never wear again.

3 His friend next door has a room at the top of her house with chests full of clothes her family has collected. They spend whole days there dressing up, as pirates, duchesses, washerwomen, spies. Sometimes, alone in the house, they wander from room to room, inventing stories about themselves, inventing selves. One afternoon they leave the house. She's chosen a cocktail dress that belonged to her mother, baggy at the chest, red stiletto heels. He is wearing a long gypsy skirt and a sort of bonnet that covers much of his face. If anyone stops them, they'll say he's her long-lost American aunt, but no one does. That evening, his father forbids him to see her and won't say why.

4 It's July but he still won't take his blazer off. The playground is used by the first three forms; there are ninety boys in all. He is one of the youngest. They all have the same school uniform, grey trousers, white shirt, brown blazer with the brown-and-yellow badge, and yellow-and-brown striped tie. Even the socks have a brown-and-yellow stripe around the top. At morning break they're allowed to remove their blazers and tuck their ties into their shirts, but he stands at the edge and watches the other boys in their white shirts and grey trousers, the younger ones like him still in shorts, and he won't take his blazer off. He feels safer with it on. He is sweating.

5  He roots through his mother's clothes until he finds one of her tops, a fine wool crew-neck pullover, salmon pink, identical to one Keith Richards is wearing in the November number of his Rolling Stones fan club magazine. He holds it against himself in front of his mother's dressing-table mirror, then takes it into the bathroom to try it on. It's cold, there's no heating in the house. He shivers as he takes off his shirt and pulls his vest over his head. He puts on the top. His nipples poke out like disgusting unripe strawberries. He rips the top off and screws it into a ball, throws it behind the toilet. He'll be in trouble but he doesn't care.

6  He gets a Saturday morning job at Skinner's hardware store, selling garden implements, screws and nails, buckets and brooms, household objects of various kinds. When he's saved enough he buys a pair of genuine Levi 501s, a size too large because they're supposed to shrink to fit. He gets them home and locks himself in the bathroom, fills the bathtub with water as hot as he can bear, strips to his skin, then puts on the jeans. They're hard and stiff, and so is he. He eases himself into the water, wincing at the heat. When he's lying in a cold bath, he gets out. The lower half of his body is stained indigo. The 501s hang from his hips.

7  At university he opens an account in a bookshop and another one at Austin Reed's, gentlemen's outfitters. The first things he buys with his cards are a book about the cultural revolution and a long green cashmere scarf. He twists the scarf twice round his neck, the fringed ends trailing like dangling vines. His hair is long and catches in the scarf; at night he picks out teasels of bright-green cashmere from the curls at the back of his neck, like decadent angel down. He's sitting in the college bar and saying how much he would prefer to live in China. You don't see people dressed like you in China, someone says. Really? he says, put down but also flattered.

8  Each Saturday afternoon they leave their cold water flat by the Arco della Pace. They cross the park, walking past De Chirico's stranded figures in the drained pool. They leave the Castle with the room they call the knotted room behind them and cross the square until the Duomo is to their right and they are walking into Rinascente, and Fiorucci, and the smaller shops of the Galleria, and along Via Montenapoleone. It is summer and people are dressed in the colours of sorbet and ice-cream cups in small provincial cinemas from his childhood. Pistachio. Lilac. They shop for T-shirts and jeans and belts and sweaters. It is hot, and so are they, and they have no idea how hot.

9   The night he meets his true love he's wearing a jacket he bought in a second-hand shop in Via del Governo Vecchio. It's blue check, unlined cotton, and has a retro American feel about it that makes him feel sexy and ironic. He's wearing it with a baby-blue Lacoste and a pair of chinos, the same beige as the beige in the jacket check, and Timberland boat shoes, without socks. It's a warm evening, and he's pulled up his jacket sleeves to show off his tan. It's late April. Decades later, his only memory of what his lover is wearing is a cap, the kind people wear in Greece, and a smile, and the cap will be a false memory.

10   He visits the second-hand clothes market every Sunday morning, returning home with bargains he never wears, discovering them months later behind the sofa or under the bed, still stuffed into pastel-coloured plastic bags. A woman from Naples has a stall of suits, and he goes through a period of imagining himself as the type of man who wears nothing else, filling a section of his wardrobe with suits that are too small, too large, too formal, too spiv-like, too dull to wear. One day he finds a suit made by Valentino, a grey so dark it's black, a wool so light it floats from the hand, the pockets still sewn shut. Weeks later, he wears it to his father's funeral.

3

# SEX

( OR )

*honey and wood*

*1*   He sits in the middle of the living-room carpet, piling up wooden blocks that have letters pasted on their sides while his mother watches *Emergency Ward Ten* on the black-and-white set. He's spelling out his name when one of the nurses says something about sex rearing its ugly head. He doesn't know what this means but he can tell from the odd way his mother shifts in her armchair and glances down at him that it's something bad. He waits for a moment, and then asks her why sex has an ugly head and what rearing means. She tells him he's too young to understand. When he spells the word SEKS with his blocks she takes them away from him.

*2*   Visiting his aunt's house, he plays with the daughter of the family two houses down. She drags him out of the house and into the outdoor lavatory, then lifts up her skirt and pulls down her knickers. They're supposed to be where someone can see them, he says, but she reaches for his shorts and quickly, as though she's done this before, unzips them and pushes them round his knees, then makes him sit on the lavatory. She squats on his lap, her shoulders against his jumper, and wriggles. He can't see over her head. His face is pressed into the cotton of her dress as she leans back into him. Do you like it? she says. No, he says.

*3* They're in the greenhouse. It's tomato season and they're surrounded by tomatoes when his best friend suggests they play nudist camps. They take their clothes off and then stand there not sure what to do next. They don't touch. It's hot and the smell of the tomatoes is almost overpoweringly strong. After a while, she suggests they play charades. He watches her growl, her chest as flat as his, then mount the handle of a spade the gardener has left in the corner and run with it pressed between her thighs. She puts the spade down and mimes the opening of a door. I'm a book, she says, but he can't guess which one. He feels faint. Everything looks red.

*4* Some weeks later they're in her playroom, at the top of the house. This time they both take off their clothes and get into bed. It's a single bed, beneath the window. They lie there, shivery at first and then hot. She pushes his head down under the sheets until his mouth is on her tummy, then further down. There's a sprinkling of hair he doesn't expect, which tickles him and makes him want to laugh, but he's scared as well. Kiss me, she says, and he does. Harder, she says, but he doesn't know what she means. He struggles back up until he can see his watch. It's time for *Five O'Clock Club*, he says. I have to go.

*5* They stand in the tent his father bought for him, a tall square tent like the kind you see in films about knights in armour. They all have their jeans around their ankles. The tent is made of some orange material. One of them has a handful of pigeon feathers. The boys push the hard end of the feathers into the ends of their dicks until they stick. The girls put the hard ends into their slits. They wriggle their hips to make the feathers move from side to side. He's told them it's what Red Indians do, to show they belong to the tribe. Their skins are bathed in orange. They're sweating. One of the girls starts to cry.

*6* It's a sleepover with one of his friends from school. They've been put in the same bed, a double bed, with a bolster and a quilted eiderdown. They start off in their pyjamas, but his friend waits until the house is quiet, then asks him if he's still asleep. No, he says. Neither am I, says his friend. They lie together, listening to each other breathe. It's hot, his friend says, and takes off his pyjama jacket. He sits up to do it, his slim bare chest turned silver by the moonlight. That's better, he says. He gets out of bed and slips his pyjama trousers off, then gets back in. Aren't you hot? he says. His hand is hard.

7   It's the afternoon of the boat race. His father wants them to watch it together, but he goes upstairs and lies on his bed. After a while, he opens his fly and reaches in, stroking himself until he's hard. He carries on stroking and something strange happens, like soft white feathers pushing to come out. For a moment, he thinks he's about to pee, to burst with pee, and will flood the bed, but then he's moaning and he has some white stuff on his belly. He's so excited he runs downstairs. He wants to tell his mother, but his father catches him in the hall, and he has time to reconsider. You missed a grand race, his father says.

8   He's in the common room, between classes. One of the boys is being picked on by a group of other boys for being cocky. He keeps his head down, he doesn't want to get involved. He's had his eye on the boy for some time. Short blondish hair, solidly built. He's never spoken to him, but he has had a dream in which the boy's dick looks like honey and a piece of polished wood all at once, and he is stroking it. When they wrestle him to the ground, his shirt comes out of the waistband and his torso arches back, bare-bellied, taut. The whole world and his heart are blinded by the light of the boy's white skin.

**9**   He buys *Health & Efficiency* from a newsagent's where he isn't known. He cuts out his favourite images of men and sticks them into last year's Stoke Arts Festival programme, alongside the underwear pages from out-of-date catalogues, a photograph of Kevin Keegan, shirtless, running across an empty field, a smaller photograph, scissored from the paper, of the dark one from *Starsky & Hutch* dressed up as Houdini, wearing chains around his neck and wrists, and not much else. He's hiding a new copy of *H&E* in his satchel the day his mother tells him about a piece of pig's liver in some friend's fridge, so riddled with cancer it wrapped itself around the milk. For the protein, she adds darkly.

**10**   He's sitting in the back of the car, reading *Brideshead Revisited* when he hears the thwack of a leather ball against a bat. He glances up. His father is driving through a village and he sees a game of cricket being played. He hates cricket, but he has a vision of waiting beneath a tree, a willow tree perhaps, with a hamper of sandwiches and champagne, and his friend is walking towards him, his bat beneath his arm, his cheeks flushed. He flops onto the picnic rug and his hair falls into his eyes as he reaches across, his hand barely brushing the knee of his friend, his lips slightly parted, his words the merest whisper. And so they come.

TRAVEL

OR

*a harp embedded*

*1*  They're driving home from the Isle of Wight. He's never crossed the sea before and, although he knows the Isle of Wight is part of England, it's as though he's been abroad. His father has the radio on. Today's the World Cup final and England is playing, but, maybe because he still feels foreign, he's secretly siding with Germany. His father is getting excited, his sister is playing with crayons and paper, his mother is talking about finding somewhere to eat. He closes his eyes. They stayed in the Hotel Metropole and had a room with a balcony overlooking the sea. He made friends with a boy from London. When England wins, he shrugs. He knows he'll go abroad again.

*2*  His first time in London his father takes him because he has work to do there. They go by train, the longest journey he's made that isn't in a car. He sits by the window and stares at the world, wondering what London will be like. When they arrive, his father takes him to Madame Tussaud's. Years later, he remembers nothing of this, nothing of the waxworks or the chamber of horrors, only the train ride, which never seemed to end, and then the long wait outside the Planetarium, because his father had said he wouldn't be long. But he is, and when he finally arrives there's no time left to see anything, and his father keeps saying, I'm sorry.

*3* They borrow a car and drive until early light, then sleep for half-an-hour in a Cornish lay-by. They have an ounce of dope and a two-man tent in the boot. They're turned away from an empty campsite, but find an abandoned field and pitch their tent, then smoke large quantities of dope. Each night two of them take the tent and the third sleeps in the car. Neither option is less uncomfortable than the other. On the last night, in a pub, he has a friendship-shaking argument with one of the other two about the value of risk. Later, he walks to the edge of the cliff and sees a harp embedded in the rock. He climbs down towards it.

*4* They sit on their rucksacks in a lay-by in Harris. It is Sunday and all the cars are driving into the town they are trying to leave, for church. They have used trains, coaches, other people's cars, a ferry and their feet to get here and the only book he still has left to read is *Don Juan*. They stand up and start to walk across a wilderness that reminds him of that canvas by Holman Hunt, of the scapegoat crowned in red. Last night the wind blew fat from their chip-shop haggis in horizontal ribbons. This morning they have eaten nothing because there can be no cooked breakfast on the day of rest. It is probably about to rain.

5　The first flight he ever takes is to Milan. It is a charter flight; some of the seats face backwards, like a train, an arrangement he will never see again. The food is dreadful but exciting; the drink is free and plentiful. He has a sick bag, which he folds and slides into his pocket when no one is looking. He stands in the bathroom, too cramped to turn, and flushes the lavatory experimentally to see what will happen, if some bright hole will open up in the plane itself. He stares through the window and wonders if what he sees are the Alps or some artful film projected onto the walls of a hangar as big as the world.

6　A friend tells him a story about a train journey she made with her boyfriend. It's a compartment train, with seats that pull out into beds. They're sharing the compartment with a Greek man, on holiday in Italy. They pull the seats out and settle to sleep, his friend in the middle. She can't sleep; she can feel the heat of the two men's bodies each side of her. When her boyfriend starts to snore, the Greek man turns and touches her breast. She lies there, silent, willing him on. He rolls on top of her and they fuck as the train heads south. It was wonderful, she says. I'll never forget the smell of him, like honey and thyme.

7  The taxi picks them up in a square so full of cicadas they can barely hear each other speak. The taxi driver thinks they're both Italian, and they don't correct him. In heavily-accented but fluent English, he talks to them about women, how Scandinavian women have cleaner private parts than women in Greece. He wants to know what women in Italy are like 'down there'. They're vague. He has a Swedish mistress he tells them, she comes each summer. She is very clean 'down there'. The following day they see him with a woman who is clearly his wife. He spots them, turns away. There are cicadas here too. They are tired of pretending. They'd like to be at home.

8  They stop for the night on Route 66, in a motel that claims to be the oldest motel in Williams. That morning they'd brunched in T-shirts outside a place near Phoenix. Now they are sitting inside a run-down room with snow banked up outside the door. They have eaten rib-eye steak and baked potatoes in a restaurant with a life-sized plaster cow outside the door. The bathroom has rusty water and the bed dips in the middle. They lie there, breathing slowly in the high thin freezing air, thinking of their lives and what has brought them here. Three rooms down, their dear friend and companion on the trip, a single woman, sits fully dressed all night, facing the door.

9 He is in a bar with a blind made of faded plastic strips at the door to keep out flies. The blind's knotted back on itself, so that one or two flies penetrate the semi-darkness to buzz around the scuffed plastic dome protecting the last third of a crumbling sponge cake. There is no other food; it's far too hot to eat. The light outside the bar is intense. A dog of indeterminate breed is lying halfway beneath one of the three zinc-topped tables squeezed under the shelter of the station eaves, each with its plastic ashtray advertising Crodino. The barman, a middle-aged man in pressed black trousers and a vest, has all the information he will ever need.

10 They have planned a fortnight in Paris, but his mother falls ill and they come back to England to be with her. They are in Cologne when his father's health fails, and they find a flight home. They are sitting in the bar of their hotel in Madrid when his partner's father is taken to hospital. They are holidaying in the valley of the shadow of death. They cancel everything to be with his mother and travel becomes what it once had been, when he was a child and there was nothing beyond the walls of the house, and within it everything, a weight and a lightness, miraculous as the weight of metal in the infinite lightness of the air.

THE BODY

OR

*this alien being*

*1*  Sometimes he wakes up at night and his arm has gone dead.
He lifts it with his working hand and moves it across his
body like a Geiger counter. He lets it rest on his stomach
and his chest, his legs and face. He lets it touch his lips to
see what it feels like to be touched in this way. He strokes
his balls, then bends the senseless fingers around his penis,
already hard, to learn about the body from outside, to see
what it must be like to be held by someone else, who is not
dead, as his arm is, but alive to him and to his needs. He
wishes his arm would stay dead for ever.

*2*  He wakes up in his own bed but the weight of the blankets
is too much for him and he can't move. He calls out for his
mother. The next thing he knows he's in his parents' bed
and the doctor is poking him, tapping his knees and ankles
with a metal hammer, asking him what he feels and if it
hurts. Nothing, he says, and no. He's looking at the ceiling,
the central light, the lampshade the colour of skin, the
fringe around its bottom, the crack that runs from one
corner of the room to the other. He is given enormous pills
to take. His mother holds his hand. Can you still feel me?
she wants to know.

3   They're standing in a line in the corridor outside the infir-
mary. They're in their underpants, the girls are somewhere
else. It's cold and some of them are shivering. He has goose
pimples on his arms. The back of the boy in front of him
has a birthmark the shape of a strawberry, with a single hair
growing out from the heart of it. He wonders if the boy
knows. Some boys have nicer underpants than others. The
boys go into the room in groups of three and leave from
another door further down the corridor. They don't look
back. He's been told there's a nurse inside, who'll touch his
balls and ask him to cough, but he doesn't believe it.

4   His uncle and aunt from Australia are staying with them.
It's summer, which means it's winter where they come from,
his uncle tells him a hundred times. He has a loud voice
and large rough hands. The boy can tell his mother doesn't
like him, and he doesn't like him either. His wife is fat and
sad, she doesn't know where to put herself. She's wearing
flowery dresses that are too tight round the waist. One
morning, as he's walking past the breakfast table, his uncle
grabs him by the elbow and twists him round to face away
from them all. Just look at the size of that arse, he says.
He's more like a girl than a bloody boy.

5   He is standing in front of his mother's mirror in his parents' bedroom. It's another house, the house with the piano and the cowboy wallpaper. His room doesn't have a mirror this big, so he's sneaked in here from the bathroom with only a towel wrapped round him. He'll say he heard a noise if anyone comes. His heart is beating hard in his chest. He's thin, bony even, his arms are like stalks. He drops the towel to the floor and stares at this alien being before him. He watches the belly-button moving in and out as he breathes. He tucks his penis and balls between his legs and imagines what it must be like to be a girl.

6   In the showers after football, some boys wander around naked, some don't. He's one of the wary ones, who sit on the benches, easing their mud-caked shirts over their heads, pretending to tease out knots in the laces of their boots while the other boys, taller and bigger and stupid, strip off their kit and slap each other's backs, then disappear into the steam. No one lets his eyes drift down to below the waist, where the mystery of them bobs and swells. He sits there, waiting to be told to strip, noticing which boy has hair, which not, wishing his own would hurry up and grow. Each body is strange to him, and frightening, his own most of all.

7. He has just been blown by an older man in a dark suit, with sunglasses, who spat his semen into a handkerchief, which he folded and put back into his pocket. The older man has now moved away from the bed and is sitting in an armchair across the room, one ankle resting on a knee, held by the hand that he's used to stroke the erection, to briefly caress the belly, the eyes still hidden behind the glasses, his own trousers readjusted. He's waiting for the next act, the part where the body he's just known more intimately than anyone else has, ever, gets out of bed and dresses in front of him. He's waiting for the final defloration.

8. He was thin for years, until he began to use a gym. He took up running, pounding out miles each week, his head filled with dreams of Marathon. He remade himself into something he might want to own, not only from within but from outside, an object worth having, possessing. This was the period of photographs in front of mirrors, when photographs had to be developed, and limits observed. He's wearing shorts in them, underpants sometimes, a singlet in one or two. His face is hidden behind the camera, but that's all right. His face isn't part of the general effect he's after. He's cutting out what's not required. What he's after, at its heart, is *ripped*. As in *out*.

**9** There's a woman comedian he sees who talks about getting married and how she's finally allowed to *eat*. It's never that conscious – what is? – but love, when it comes, has a similar effect. The body he's seen as mystery, and then as shame, and lastly as value, becomes a place in which they can both relax, a haven. They hold each other's substance. When his father says he's developing a belly, he's briefly annoyed, but moves on. His father is the same weight he was when he was twenty. His mother has fought a constant battle with her waistline, as people say. He'll be his own man, he decides, and his partner's. He'll eat what's given him and be glad.

**10** His parents bathed him as a child. His body was theirs, flesh of their flesh, he had no secrets. His vomit, his shit, his arms reaching out, shampoo in his eyes, his tears, his blood to be wiped off, his wounds to be healed, the good-night kiss. And then came the parting, and his body spun off like a moon into some dark space they could only infer from that absence. And then, because the most natural form is the orbit, he finds himself holding his father's hand and wiping his mouth and his arse, and his mother is a child in his arms, her trust, her willingness, her need in his like the meeting of a hook and eye.

DANGER

**OR**

*all that sweetness*

*1*  They cycle out to a place about five miles from the village where the lane, little more than the width of a car, curves round to the right. At the side is the steeply sloping grass verge and, at the top of the verge, a metal fence. He hooks his bare legs round the lowest rung of the fence and lets himself down until he is dangling with his forehead no more than a foot from the soft summer tarmac of the road. The others sit along the top rail of the fence, waiting. Straining up, he can see the soles of their sandals. When the first car hurtles past him the rush of air is like an adult's slap.

*2*  They stand around the pool in their winter clothes, scarves tucked into their woollens, their feet in wellingtons. The first child walks out onto the ice, and then the second. The pool, or pit as it's known, is in a hollow, bare trees all round it. No one can see them, no one can hear them call. He joins the other two. Together they edge their way towards the centre of the pit. Beneath their feet, the ice is cloudy, irregular, less white than he's expected, stripped branches trapped within it. He sees what looks like a harp, a doll, an uncle's face, a deepness. With a rustle like fire, the crack comes running across the ice to greet them.

*3*  He is cycling home from school along the narrow lane when a car overtakes too close. He swerves into the verge. Some long dried grasses catch in the wheel and tangle among the spokes. Continuing to pedal, he bends down over the handlebars to disentangle them, tugging as the front wheel wobbles from side to side. The grasses hold. He reaches further in, as close to the spinning wheel as he can get. Before he knows it his hand is caught between spokes and fork and acts as a brake. He is thrown like a doll across and down and in front of his own bicycle, which tears at his back as his forehead skids along the road. Blood, blind.

*4*  She closes both eyes as soon as the bicycle begins to move at speed. She freewheels down the hill, the road the narrowest ribbon beneath her feet, a great rush and a darkness, a counting as far as she dares before she opens them. She is shaking with the wonder of her courage and the risk of it. Forty years later her son sits in a car at night, the lights turned off, and he is driven along a fen road, straight as a die, his eyes half-open, half-closed, by a woman whose eyes are entirely closed, and they are both laughing as hard as they can until she pulls up at the kerb and is sick into her lap.

5  The side door to the college is locked and it's too late to slip through the porter's lodge. They try to climb over an iron railing but one of them loses his footing and cuts a hand. Then they remember the underground car park with a second exit inside the college. They hurry down the piss-stained stairs and through the door. The first one's already stumbling when someone hits the light switch and they're standing at the edge of a moaning carpet of men in cast-off clothes and sacking, a groping carpet that struggles to its feet as they gather together and shrink in fright, the noise of men stirring into life and their own noise, echoing, bleeding into one.

6  He snorts coke with strangers and they are his wonderful friends until they split and he sobs alone in the middle of a street he has never knowingly understood. One friend drops a tab beneath a cliff on a beach on the island, too scared to move in case the cliff crumbles onto his head. Another friend flies from a terrace but forgets to remind the road to take him in, to hold him, his arms outstretched in excess of love. A third friend shares heroin in a stranger's flat in a border town. It's his only time. He is struck by jaundice, then dies. His final joke. If I'd been yellow, I'd never have known what being yellow means.

7   It is early morning, summer. The air smells of evergreen, some kind of laurel perhaps, leaves crushed into fragrance by backs and knees and cheeks. A cry of help comes out of a bush and he walks in to see a small man with his trousers round his ankles and a teenage boy with a knife. He wants my wallet, says the man. The boy stands there, uncertain what to do, watching as the intruder eases the knife from his hand. You don't need this, he says. This is a place of love. He closes the knife, gives it back to the boy and walks out of the bush. The small man, in white clogs, follows him home. He's scared.

8   He has sex with men whose names he doesn't know and doesn't ask. He's bent over in parks and fucked by more men than one, and pushed to his knees by these and others. He carries them home on his moped, too drunk to steer. He climbs into parked cars and sucks off the driver to stay out of the sudden summer rain, hands pressing his dripping hair into the driver's groin. He's blown by an older man who works in a sugar factory – all that sweetness – who tells him his life is shit, the world is shit, but whose cock is as smooth, and hard, and warm as polished wood. He has never worn a condom in his life.

**9** He has lunch with friends in his favourite restaurant. They eat seafood and drink white wine on a wooden platform raised above the beach, behind a bank of succulents with star-like flowers, the acid pastels of love hearts. Between the table and the sea, the rows of blue-and-white striped umbrellas have been taken down and furled like leaves against an unexpected wind. They order more wine and then, when the meal is over, and a final glass of grappa has been drunk, he stands up and jumps from the platform, half-walks, half-runs towards the abandoned sea, taking off his T-shirt and kicking his sandals from his feet, two waiters close behind. He falls like bright rain into the moon-swayed waves.

**10** His home is on fire, the telephone fused into a molten lump of red and grey, the part that rings out still ringing. He stands beside the burning house, his hands in his pockets, and the air is filled with scraps of paper on which he has written his secret truths, now curling and blackened and lost even to him. The world smells of petrol and fat and the ringing of the phone is dulled by the sharp bark of a dog, his mother's dog, stifled by smoke as it scrapes against the concrete larder floor to hide its final bone. Nowhere is safe. The ringing goes on, and the dog's bark, and his secrets, filigreed by the cajoling flame.

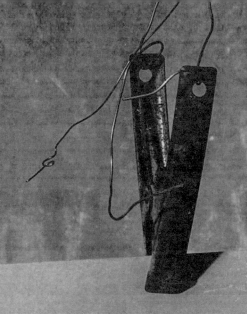

ANIMALS

7

OR

*the whelp of an alien god*

*1*   The first animal in his life to die is Sandy, a retriever brought
down by a barbed wire fence. He has no memory of this.
What he remembers is a woman with a tweed skirt and a
terrier of some sort, or possibly an untrimmed poodle, and
this dog, whose breed he can't quite place, attacking him
as they stand outside a post office in the village he started
school in, and his being afraid, and possibly bitten, as he
has never been afraid of any dog before or since. And then
he remembers swans in the park lake by the library and his
mother telling him they can break a grown man's leg with
one sweep of their wing.

*2*   He's presented with three white mice in a plywood box,
divided by a wall with a zero at its heart. The smaller part
has newsprint shredded for bedding, the larger an exercise
wheel and canisters for food and water. The front of the
box is panelled with glass. He hopes his mice will breed,
holding them belly up to see what sex they are, but all he
can see are pimple-like bumps. When he goes on holiday
he forgets to leave food and water for them. He is too
ashamed to say. Back home, heart beating, he runs to the
box. Curled up in a corner, pink as marshmallow beneath
the bedding, he finds a half-eaten cluster of baby mice.

*3*   His father comes home one day, carrying a dog bought from some passing stranger, who was beating it with a stick because it had misbehaved. Don't touch it, his father says. Not yet. The dog shakes as his father places it in the armchair nearest the fire, its lips drawn back. Its name is Rascal. A crossbreed with brown eyes, it's soon his father's shadow. It settles, sleeps by the hearth, is loved. One day it catches a rat. Good Rascal, his father says, good boy. With other people, it backs off, darts forward to nip their bums, a nip that's half-bite, half-suck. Its last day alive it draws bright blood from the thigh of a child with a stick.

*4*   He goes to a country grammar school with a farm attached. He watches the pink-white udders of cows being drained and hens' necks lightly wrung. In biology lessons they're given live frogs to take apart, one frog between two. With the end of his four-coloured biro, he prods at the grey beating heart, exposed, a sick smile on his face, the smell of ether still in the air, then wires the back legs to a battery and watches them twitch. Later, they stand round the pen where the pigs are kept and the pig-man picks up each of the piglets and slices off his testicles, the size and shape of baked beans, and the piglets squeal out their little hearts.

5 When they buy a cottage in the Pennines, a dog and two cats are part of the deal. The cats disappear before nightfall but Susie stays. She's been chained her whole life in the hollowed-out carcase of a rusted car, but they're townsfolk, they let her into the house. She skirts the walls, then curls in a corner to sleep. On heat, she disappears for days and nights together. When the litter's born, the final pup is rose-grey, misshapen, over twice the size of the rest, a parody of a runt, the whelp of an alien god. Susie snuffles at it, anxious. She watches the man bear it off to the bucket, then turns to the other pups with relief.

6 He's coming out of the Arcady, alone, when he sees the dog. It's four o'clock, almost dawn. He can't afford a taxi. The club's on the outskirts of the city, and he's tired and sad. The dog keeps its distance as he sets off, walking through areas of boarded-up warehouses, residential streets, closed shops, closed schools, closed metro stations. He notices a bar about to open for people setting up a nearby market and stands outside until the coffee machine's turned on. The dog sidles over and presses its muzzle into his hand. You can't come home with me, he says, stroking the dog's head. I haven't got any home to go to. The dog nods, understanding, and slips away.

7   They're walking down the hill towards the beach when she
sees a cat on the wall and stops to stroke it. She's drunk;
they both are. He walks on a little, watching the full moon
reflected on the sea, until he hears her call. She's standing
with her hand on the cat's back and a man beside her. She's
wearing a white top that picks up the light of the moon.
Come back and rescue me, she says, and the man turns to
look at him, then backs away. He walks back up the hill to
where she's standing, the man moving off against the wall.
He says the cat's his mother, she says. He nods. He must
be mad.

8   She's sitting in a cardboard box with the word FREE in felt
tip on the flap. The last thing they need is a dog, they've
barely unpacked, but she fits so neatly into his hand, her
small legs dangling from his palm, her head the size of a
small round apple, peach-furred to the touch. They decide
to take her home. Apart from her belly, which is palest pink
and human, she's the colour of toffee. They call her Toffee.
One ear lies flat against her head, the other refuses. They
could watch her all day as she stumbles and sits on her
haunches, eternally surprised, or tries to climb down the
step from the kitchen. Some days, they do.

**9** They stumble across a zoo in a park behind a mosque. It's a sad place and the saddest place of all is the cage with the orang-utans inside. One of them has been here for fourteen years, they read on a card, and it's a life sentence and the orang-utan in question, picking at her teeth with a slim pink-fronted finger, knows this and is asking them what she's done to deserve it and if they can put her in touch with a clever lawyer. They walk into another room half-filled with branches. After a moment he sees the sloth, only feet away from him and looking at him with upside-down sympathy and asking him what he's done, and why.

**10** His mother falls ill and they hurry to be with her, leaving Toffee at home in the care of a friend. There is death all round them, parents, parents of friends; the cat they rescued from an empty terrace was buried in the cork wood only months before, wrapped in a small white towel, the claggy earth on the spade relentless as memory. Days pass, the nurse says full moons carry people off, staring meaningfully at the grey-blue light in the sky. They sit beside his mother but the next day, his mother still alive, they hear that Toffee is ill, then worse, then dead. They sit beside his mother while friends take her beautiful corpse to the cork wood.

LANGUAGE

OR

*death and cucumbers*

*1*   No one remembers his first words. While his mother is expecting him she holds her mouth in a certain way, so that his mouth will be like hers, a full mouth, firm but soft, her tongue held curled within it, slowly to be shared as the two of them speak to each other in the otherwise silent house. She hates baby words, forbids them in his presence. He will never have a bow-wow or hear a moo-cow. He learns to read as soon as he can hold a book in his hands. Before that, he traces the word *mother* on her forearm while she reads him a bedtime story, his fingernail tickling out the letters he has conjured from air.

*2*   He loves big words, the way they snake and bend. Some words are silky smooth, like Blancmange; others are jointed, like Articulate. He learns and remembers the botanical names for red hot poker and convolvulus and is called on to repeat them to family friends, who smile and applaud. He hears, and learns, the word Precocious, like Precious with a secret at its heart. He whispers new words to himself to see how they feel in his mouth, how they sound in his ear. Some words, like Fruit and Awful, are rounder than others. Quick is quick, Slow, slow. Teasing his sister, he confuses Osculate with Copulate and causes a brief scandal in the car. His favourite word is Awkward.

*3* He makes mistakes. His first mistake is to think that Misle is a verb, rhyming with pizzle, although he won't know the word pizzle for many years, its past tense regular, meaning to side-track or derail. He tells his teacher he's been misled, rhyming it with fizzled, and can't understand why everyone laughs. His second mistake is to use the word Unyet, a word he is sure he has heard a hundred times on other people's lips, but cannot write without his teacher underlining it in red. His third mistake is to think he can suit his words to those around him; that what marks him out can also be used to blend him in. So many mistakes, unyet. Unyet.

*4* His first friend to die is called Tony Hand and all he can think about as they sit in the assembly hall to be told is that the name is like three parts of the body. Toe. Knee. Hand. He looks at his own hands, resting on his knees, and thinks about what it must be like to be dead. He lies in bed and names the parts of his body with new words, to protect himself and them, starting at Foot and working up to Hair. His word for Tongue is Icicle. Later that week, he attends the funeral at church. He's cold. He can see his breath. Icicle is the wrong word, but it's too late to change.

5   They wait until her parents are out before playing the game, in the drawing room. Nervous, they stumble over words, try hard not to giggle. But soon, sipping their cocktails and lighting another cigarette, the people they have chosen to be taken over by, step by step, direct their words and gestures, the path their conversation follows. They are foreign to themselves; they can barely imagine what it must be like to be children, playing games in a drawing room. The longer they use the new words the easier it is to understand that everything they have said before has been a lie. They have always known this language. There is nothing else. They fall silent, too scared to speak.

6   It pleases him that Spell is how the word is made but also, in the hands of the magician, how the world is changed. One letter separates Word from World and that letter is like the number one, or an 'I', or a shaft of light between almost closed curtains. There is an old letter called a thorn, which jags and tears at the throat as it's uttered. Later he learns that Grammar and Glamour share the same deep root, which is further magic, and there can be neither magic without that root, nor plant. He's lost in it like Chid in Child, or God reversed into Dog. Somewhere inside him is a colon. A sentence can last for life.

7 He's buying a name tag for Tilly, his cat, in the next town up the coast. He sits in the shop while the tag's engraved, surrounded by medals and trophies, sports cups, the names and dates of the dead. The shopkeeper asks him where he's from. England, he says. You're Protestant? she says. He shakes his head. I'm atheist, he says. She's startled. You mean you don't believe in God? she says. How can you not believe in God? He's bored. He shrugs. She says, You must believe in something. I do, he says. I believe in this chair. I believe in death and cucumbers. I believe in my cat's name, Jeoffry. I believe that every living thing is holy.

8 He dreams of waking in a foreign city in which he has lived for almost all his life and no longer speaking the language of that city. He looks at his partner beside him, in the bed they have shared for more than twenty years and there is nothing he can say, no way he can tell him what has happened. When his partner wakes and speaks, he shakes his head and the words that come out of his mouth are baby words. *Baa-baa. Choo-choo.* Words denied him as a child. His partner continues to speak, but nothing he says makes sense. He wakes in the bed he has dreamt of only moments before. He opens his mouth to speak.

9   He finds himself translating a book about the philosophy of listening, and it strikes him that what he is doing as he translates is precisely that; he is listening, as if through a wall, his ear pressed up to the text as though it were paper and plaster, and beyond the plaster some rigid lightweight but sustaining structure, possibly of wood, and beyond that a second skin of plaster and paper, and the passage inward moving outward, repeated in reversed order, a room full of people who are talking all together about listening, and about their demons, because not only Socrates had his demon, to whom he listened. Sometimes there is so much noise the book is hard to hear.

10   He is watching his father die in hospital. His father is explaining to him that he must call for a taxi to take him home. He gives him a piece of paper with an address that has never existed, a collage of all the houses they have owned, a magical home from which he has been exiled to die. He listens to his father repeat the address time and again, and each time it is different. The final effect is kaleidoscopic. The last day of his life, still in hospital, he asks his son to fetch him something, but the word is incomprehensible and his son, faced by his father's deafness, is reduced to miming out what it might be.

MONEY

OR

*brown sauce sandwiches*

*1*　He has no first memory of money. There is no primal scene in which he reaches into a pocket, or wallet, or purse, or finds himself exchanging something of no apparent worth – mere paper and metal – for something he wants. It's as invisible as language, it pre-dates consciousness, it is simply there. Yet his earliest memories of his parents arguing are memories of arguments based around money, his moving from house to house, from school to school; a moving spurred on by money and its absence. It's as powerful, and invisible, and all-encompassing as God must once have seemed and yet at no point can he remember thinking, So this is what money is, this is what money can do.

*2*　They find a stash of empty pop bottles beneath the sink in the scullery of the half-timbered house near the church, abandoned for years, the bare rooms filled with traces of sheltering tramps. There must be a hundred at least, some with labels and some without. They work it out. Three pence a bottle makes twenty-five shillings, a fortune. He brings his wheeled cart and together they load the bottles into it; it takes them a good half-day to rinse them out in her garden shed. They carry them to the pub, the only place they can collect the deposit. The landlady looks at the bottles as they're lifted and stacked on the counter, then looks at them. They wait.

*3* He's waiting for his father to get home, standing on the sofa beside the bay window that looks onto the street. When the car comes round the corner he waves and jumps up and down. His father drives past the window and beneath the arch that leads into the yard, then storms into the house. He's furious. He walks across the room and grabs the arm of his son, who's still on the sofa, and pulls him off until the boy is half-standing, half-crouching on the floor. His father slaps him round the back of the head. By the time his mother comes in they're both shaking. That sofa's new, his father says. He must think I'm made of money.

*4* When his mother buys a shop he's introduced to the idea of credit, or 'tick'. He learns that some people are good for credit and others aren't, and that those who most need it, people who live on brown sauce sandwiches and have budgerigars flying free in their lounges, are those who most often are denied it. His mother says this can't be helped. His father says money doesn't grow on trees, but it seems to him that those with trees are those who have money, and that those whose gardens are filled with broken prams and dog shit and no trees are those who need credit, and don't get it. Maybe his father is wrong. Maybe they're all wrong.

5  His father collects old pennies. He has a boxful, some of them older than he is, curved and worn thin and black as coal, and a book containing lists of their values. Some pennies, he says, are like stamps, like Penny Blacks, and are worth more than they say they're worth, as though some magic has been done on them. They have their own value and another, magical value, and his father has the book of spells that confers this value. Each night, he polishes his coins and organises them into piles, then checks them against the book. He's too busy to talk to anyone. He's convinced that one day he will find the penny that will change their lives.

6  A friend of his becomes obsessed by one-armed bandits. He spends whole evenings in the Castle, his bitter glass balanced on the top of the machine as it shakes and whirls its unholy trinity, as it eggs him on, his spirited and unlikely partner, until he can feed it no longer. His aunt was also addicted to fruit machines, her pension, and then her house, devoured by them. But he's never been taken in by gambling; convinced of his natural luck, he won't have that conviction dented. When he buys a lottery ticket and doesn't win, it's as if he's lost something already his. He feels both cheated and incredulous, betrayed in his way as his aunt was in hers.

7 He's going through some old papers when he finds a manila envelope from his university days. It's full of cheques, from the days when a bank would give its customers back each cheque they'd signed. It's the nearest thing he possesses to a diary of those years. The sums are small, often no more than a pound, and the frequency more or less daily. It's a pity they don't have the time they were cashed. He'd bet now most of them were scribbled and taken to the bank next door to his college at some point between three and three fifteen. And so his day would start, as he learned the value of money by signing its mystery into life.

8 His first year in Milan, in the city's shops and bars, he's given scraps of paper bearing the names of one-branch banks from southern towns, dirty and creased, their colours smudged. Like toffees and telephone tokens, they're standing in as change. The coins they replace have been recycled as the backs of cheap wristwatches, or melted down into their component metals. These so-called *mini-assegni* are tokens of trust in as pure a sense as can be imagined. When that trust fails, what you have is shabby confetti, only redeemed by travelling to the constellation of single banks that issued them, a thousand kilometres south. One day, you take the train, your pockets stuffed with paper as the bare heat builds.

*9* For five months, waiting for his first salary, he lives on a roll with jam for breakfast, a roll with cheese for lunch and a plate of spaghetti with garlic and tomato sauce for dinner. Each day he drinks a half-litre of milk and a litre of local wine. He's worked out that he can live like this for the rest of his life. He buys his rolls and cheese from the grocer's beneath the flat and his wine from the *enoteca* opposite. He's thrilled by the way he looks in photos, like a dissident in a gulag. He dreams about money the way other people dream about alien abductions. When he's paid he stands in the street and cries.

*10* His horoscope says he'll experience periods of wealth and periods of poverty. He doesn't believe in horoscopes, but, deep down, he does believe, just as he doesn't believe in money, but deep down, he does believe; he has no choice but to believe. He feels the protection money can offer and then withhold until he's learned some useful lesson. He puts his hand in a pocket one day and finds a five pound note when it's needed. He's the only person around one August to take on a job that changes his life. He doesn't save. He hopes. He likes the story about the two loaves of bread, how one loaf is eaten, and the other exchanged for a flower.

# THEFT

**OR**

*uniformly golden*

*1*  One morning, he takes a ten shilling note from his mother's handbag. He cycles into the next village and buys ten No. 6 'for his aunt'. On his way out of the shop, he's spotted by his aunt, on her way into the shop. She asks him what he's up to so far from home. Nothing, he says and gets on his bike. Halfway back, he throws the packet of cigarettes into the ditch. He cycles another quarter mile, then flings the change from the cigarettes across the hedge into a field. His mother never notices the money is missing. His aunt never mentions seeing him. He goes back three days later, but can't find the cigarettes or the money.

*2*  They go into the fishmonger's, pretending they don't know each other. One of them asks for half a pint of whelks. While the fishmonger fetches the whelks from a fridge at the back of the shop, the other student reaches into the tank in the window and lifts out a lobster, then runs into the street with the lobster hidden beneath his jacket. Walking back to the counter, the fishmonger hears a startled yelp from outside the shop and glances at the first student with a puzzled look on his face, but doesn't notice there's a lobster missing. After they've treated the nip on the thief's hand with antiseptic, they throw the lobster into a pot and watch it die.

*3* Dawdling on his way back to the changing room after football, he's last boy out of the showers. He starts to get dressed but he can't find his underpants. The only pair he can see, lying on his bit of the bench, are some torn and greying Y-fronts, elastic gone at the waist, a fresh skid mark at the arse. Too embarrassed to say anything he waits until all the other boys have gone, then puts them on. When his mother spots them on his bedroom floor she hits the roof and calls the school. At morning assembly next day, the headmaster threatens everyone with detention until the missing underpants are returned. Everyone turns to stare at him, ashamed, humiliated.

*4* He's spent all night at the station, heaving sacks of Christmas mail from trains onto the platform. When he clocks off at six o'clock, he's coming down from a big fat line of coke and has a terrible thirst. At the bus stop, he picks up a milk bottle from a step. It's half-empty when a police car pulls up. He's arrested and charged with theft. Three and a half weeks later he's in court. He's fined six pounds and the cost of a bottle of gold top. He pays by cheque. By this time Christmas is over and he no longer has a job. He uses the summons to roll a joint that doesn't draw, however hard he sucks.

5 One afternoon, he takes his mother around town in a wheel-chair. After sharing a BLT at Costa's they go to a charity shop near the statue of Prince Albert in Queen's Square. His mother asks him to hand down all the size sixteen tops from the upper rail. He stands beside the chair and hands them down, one after the other. It's not until they leave the shop and his mother wants her compact from her handbag, which he's placed in the detachable carrier at the back of the wheelchair, that he realises the handbag's been stolen. Someone must have taken it in the charity shop while he was distracted. Some charity, the policewoman says. They ought to be shot.

6 During morning break he steals a packet of tampons from the corner shop while his friends are buying sweets and chocolate bars. Around the corner, they rip open the box and unwrap a tampon, shooting it out from the cardboard tube with gusts of laughter. At school, when everyone has seen the tampons and nobody shows any further interest, he sneaks down to the teachers' car park during lunch and ties a tampon to each of the door handles of the cars belonging to the headmaster, the deputy headmaster, both men, and the history teacher, a woman. They go down to the car park after school to see what will happen but someone has removed the tampons, and nothing does.

7  He's working at a summer school for foreign teenagers. Sorting through their washed laundry one day he finds the underpants of a boy from Como. The boy is the son of a famous industrialist, who was kidnapped once and then released. Like all the boy's clothes, these were made for him by a tailor. They are modelled on the standard Y-front design, but are hand-stitched and feel as if they contain silk. They are monogrammed across the buttoned fly. He thinks of the measuring and the boy's skin, which is uniformly golden, and has an erection. When he has sorted the rest of the students' clothes, he picks up the underpants, folds them neatly and slips them into his pocket.

8  They get the munchies one night and decide to see what they can find. Two of them sneak into a communal kitchen on the next landing up and are caught by a born-again Christian, red-handed with two eggs and a slice of cheese. They put them back where they found them, mumbling about charity, and return to their room for another joint. A quarter of an hour later, the third one reappears with an untouched quiche Lorraine on a plate. They ask him where it came from and he giggles. From inside someone's room. The next day they're having lunch in the canteen and they hear someone tell his friend about a quiche-eating ghost. He says, I'll never sleep again.

9  He's standing on a bus in Rome when he sees a good-looking
lad glancing his way. The bus is crowded. As more people
get on, he edges his way down the aisle until his thigh and
then his arse are pressed against the lad's leg. He lets the
bus jolt him against the leg as it shifts and flexes. He has
a hard-on by now. He can feel the lad's hand adjusting his
trousers, pressing against him. He pushes towards the exit,
the lad close behind him, hot and hard, exploratory. When
the bus stops he gets off and turns to smile but the lad's
not there. He's struck by a sense of loss. He checks his
back pocket. Empty.

10  The first time he waits to pay for the book, but no one
comes to the till, and he leaves with it in his hand. The
second time he slides the book into his pocket after glancing
around. After that it's simple. Soon, he begins to steals on
commission. He's crouched down with his bag open and
his hand on a book about the Hittites when some move-
ment catches his eye. He looks up and sees a man he knew,
who died three years before. The man is smiling and looking
towards another part of the bookshop. Following his eyes,
he sees a floorwalker heading his way. He puts the book
back. He leaves the shop. He never steals again.

# ART

**OR**

*human-sized quilts*

*1*  They're painting in her mother's laundry. It's a room with a washing machine and a dryer and the air is damp and warm. Kneeling together on the floor with tubes of colour and paper, neither of them is sure what to do, but her parents have paintings in the house and the pressure to produce is strong. They've acquired the idea that art is self-expression, which doesn't help. Their knees are beginning to hurt. He writes the word Pain in blue letters and then adds a 't' to make Paint. The cleaning lady comes in with a basket of dirty washing. If you haven't got anything better to do, she says, you can help me peg out the last lot.

*2*  A friend of his mother's studied art. She has a painting hanging on the landing. It's hard to say what it shows, it is colours and shapes, but he can't not look at it. He touches the surface to make sure it's real and not a print, and the paint is rough, and ridged, and alive. He lingers at the top of the stairs after using the bathroom, until his mother's friend comes to see what he's doing. Did you make this? he says. She shakes her head. Beautiful, isn't it? she says. I'd like to be an artist, he says, and make paintings like this. She strokes his hair from his forehead. Let this be our secret, she says.

3  Art class is on Tuesday afternoon. They're supposed to have drawn a pencil sketch of a pair of shoes. He's planned to tell the teacher he's forgotten his sketch pad, but two other boys before him use the same excuse, so he decides he'll risk the truth. He spent the entire weekend searching out shoes, his plimsolls with the elastic tabs, the wellington boots his father uses to clean the henhouses, his mother's court shoes with the heels too high for her to wear, his sister's Startrite sandals, but none of them inspired him enough to want to draw them. His first lesson. I didn't ask for inspiration, his teacher says, clipping him round the ear. I asked for shoes.

4  They've found a thin white book of Botticelli reproductions to copy from. They laugh about the name for a while, then start to look through the plates, the word they've learned to use for pictures. The book is part of a series called *Masters of Colour*, although the colours in this one are nothing compared to the ones in the Chagall. Chagall's stuff also looks easier to copy and they're on the point of opting for a picture of a flying mermaid when he flicks through the Botticelli a final time and sees the man with his hand on his hip reaching up into a fruit tree. He's holding what looks like a fly swatter. Let's copy this, he says.

5   He has a Pre-Raphaelite period in his mid-teens. It's the
levelling out of attention that intrigues him, as though no
leaf mattered more than any other, no person mattered
more than any leaf. It goes against what he knows of nature
so violently that he feels at home in the bright vermilion
splashes and acid green lichen of the rock where the scapegoat wanders. He lies like Ophelia herself, submerged in
improbable water, his skin indistinguishable from the
flowers, a sort of madness on him. And then, just as soon
as it came, the madness leaves him and he rises from the
water and walks back into the house, freed, focused on
some necessary thing, with everything else a haze.

6   *The Blind Leading the Blind.* He buys a poster of the Bruegel
painting for the space above his desk and sticks it up with
Blu-Tack, though he'd have preferred to have it framed.
Other people have Magritte, or Dali, or David Hamilton,
but he likes the realism of the Bruegel, its harshness and
humour, the way the faces already resemble skulls. He likes
the idea of an artist painting the image of a man who cannot
see, of a string of men. He likes the cynicism of it, and the
hopelessness. He's young enough to find pleasure in these,
and the church that no one will enter, and the fact that the
cause of each man's blindness can be identified.

7   He's introduced by a friend who makes pressings of sheets of slate to a group of Austrian artists. He hears about how they use blades and knives and ropes to break down the defences of the bourgeois body. He sees pictures of human heads disfigured by ordure, of piss and entrails and genitals. He's shocked, disturbed, alerted to desires in himself. He wants to know how art can be made irreversible by the artist's removing his own arm, his own tongue. His penis. He sees for the first time the body as a site of outrage, and of power, and then he doesn't want to know any more, and pulls away from the place they've tried to lead him into.

8   There is more than one way of being mad. He walks around an exhibition of magical writing and armies of marauding schoolgirls, of endlessly repeated vehicles of war. An artist whose work he first saw in a book his parents gave him when he was ten is now making images of cows from dust and what might be dung, and cities from the same materials, and cars and people, and they're lovely, childlike in their shameless, apparently artless engagement. And then there's Warhol and the same face over and over again, and ideas of fame that are new, although it's hard to believe that now, three decades on, with the madness at full pitch and the armies at every door.

9  The line between art and the intricate wonder of the new toy grows finer. But all is not lost. Among the medicine cabinets and the lacquered poodles, the labia and the lingam, the tangles of monumental wire, there are human-sized quilts sewn by women in territories ravaged by men's wars, and other quilts made in Margate that test the heart. Sometimes, he thinks, it's the women who most disturb; the washing, the plates, the spider a tribe could shelter under, the tights filled with foam, the cuddly toys like trophies around the neck of a soldier, penises, ears, a string of dung dyed wedding red. The whole bloody mess of the home, like a secret he has kept from himself.

10  What is it that lasts the distance? he wonders. The small stuff, maybe, paintings he has seen and not forgotten. There's a canvas he saw once, the size of a ladies handkerchief, in a show brought to Rome from the Hermitage, by Rouault, and it's stayed with him like a jewel glimpsed through a window. A single, appropriated jewel, because wherever it hangs it's his. And there are paintings he carries with him, from house to home, and objects, pocket-sized sometimes. On the back of a miniature he once found the words *He who is not consumed by love grows cold*. The truth is that he has always loved artists. He has been lucky. His art has loved him back.

WORK

**OR**

*but in the doing*

*1*  He's first aware of work as absence, his father's absence. Following that, as intrusion, living behind and above the grocer's shop his mother buys to gain her freedom. She takes on a woman to look after the children and her house, and a second woman to help her in the shop. Thus work breeds work. One day, perched on the edge of the bath, he tells his father he wants to be an entomologist. His father cuts himself shaving. Wiping the blood off, he says, Insects? That's dirty work. His mother is telling the woman who helps in the shop to cover the bacon before the flies can lay their eggs on it. He dreams about entomology, spreading his wings.

*2*  They tell the woman in the pub the pop bottles come from the back of her parents' cellar. The woman shakes her head. Madam's family don't buy their drink from here, she says. They're far too high and mighty. The girl is pulling at his sleeve but he won't give up. They've worked all morning, scrubbing bottles clean. These must have belonged to the people before, he says. In that case, the woman smirks, there's no deposit. I never charged *them*. She stares down, her eyes like dirty stinking wells for them to drown in. He separates three bottles from the others. These are mine, he says, from my house. I want my nine pence. He reaches up his hand.

3   When he thinks about his future, work plays no part. He thinks about places and people, about words and faces and foreign signs, flavours that remind him of no food he has ever tasted, of men and their bodies, and it is larger, more intense and less predictable than any work could ever be. At school, his careers officer suggests he join the army. He's scornful. He chooses the least vocational subject possible to read at university. He wins a scholarship, receives a grant. Sustenance falls from the air. On his gap year, he signs on, makes no plans, preferring freedom. His life unrolls before him, waiting to receive his feet. He's given the job of signing other people on.

4   He works in a tax office one summer, a view of bare hills from the window. He finds a corner in the archive from which to blow smoke into the air. Later, he works in another office, a shop, and then a stall. He sells fruit to foreigners at inflated prices, steals from the till. He spends what he steals in shops he will never work in, shops where handsome men offer him clothes he could never, otherwise, afford. He buys himself a snakeskin belt as thin as a whip from a shop called Castigation. He eats in fashionable restaurants, with pop stars at adjacent tables. Days later, he is scrubbing fat from oven trays in their endless, echoing kitchens.

5  There are jobs that lead nowhere but out of where he is. He applies to build schools in the Congo, but is not accepted. He's offered a job in the deserts of Arabia, deserts he will irrigate in some mysterious fashion, but his sponsor dies unexpectedly. He's called for interview by a shipping line, but gets drunk in a dockside pub and is fucked by a sailor between two bins, missing his appointment. He applies to teach in a school in another country, and is interviewed by a mad woman with a mink, who takes him on. Soon he is the only person in the room who speaks English. His students stare at him. He sets the timer and begins.

6  Places in which people work include factories, offices, restaurants, schools and fields. He has worked in all of these, except the first. He has learned he would rather work than not, and wonders if this would be true if work weren't paid. In economic theory, work is divided into the production of goods and services, but he's never produced a good that can be bartered or sold in his life, unless he himself is that good. He has proffered his services in more ways than one; his body cut and trimmed to fit. He reads about alienation and wonders, Is this me? as he dips his hands into soapy water or takes a call or adjusts his mouth to suit.

*7*  One boss treats him like an adopted son, feeds him and reads his poems and sacks him because workers' rights are nothing beside a mother's love and she has paid him with her heart. Another boss promises to listen to his complaint and do nothing but listen; days later, the man betrays his trust and destroys a friendship with a colleague. A third boss holds a gun to his head. It seems the workplace has deep, unspoken loyalties but sometimes it is hard to know what they are; they are bonds and boundaries, and he feels like the honey bee in the web of the spider, a web so large the spider can labour within it and not be seen.

*8*  He wishes he had been a dancer. He would like to have been light-footed, hard-muscled, stripped down to sinew and bone and sweat, able to carry another man across a stage as though there were nothing in the world that could not be lifted, his body an instrument of his will, his will the instrument of an art that has life in that moment and no other, the weight and the weightlessness enhancing and denying each other within the circle of a single blue-white spotlight, and, beyond that, darkness and silence. He would like to have been tired and aching and fit for purpose. He would like to have woken up alone and found himself surrounded by roses and applause.

**9** For each day worked there is a price to pay, but no one has told him what it is, nor where it goes, nor whose purpose it serves. It's a slow drip that might be used to torture him if it wasn't so benign, so inevitable, such a trivial amount it's barely noticed. It's taken, a drop from a vein on the inside of the arm, or gradually scraped from the softer tissue of the mouth or the surface of the tongue; it might be a hair of the head or the stomach, a particle of nail so small it disappears into the wax as soon as it's dipped. Until the wax hardens and the doll he is is forged.

**10** His work is the only thing that counts. One work after another until they are *works, collected*, his name on the spine. He had a friend who began his collected works as a boy by writing the contents page, beginning with *juvenilia*, which he set himself to compose; but his heart wasn't in it. Already, the real work had been done. The one true work is the one that works something out, uncertain what it is, working in darkness, working the inside out. Outside the circle of light is the darkness and silence of a mine and there is no telling what the mine may hold. What's mine is yours. There is no sense to work but in the doing.

MUSIC

13

*the global studio*

*1*  He's sitting in the back of the car with his mother and sister. His godfather, in the front beside his father, who is driving, is singing a song he's never heard before. His god-father has a baritone voice, he finds out when he learns the names of voices, and he is singing about a kid with a drum and the building of towers, and about railroads, and about dimes. He wants to know what dimes are but his mother tells him to hush. And then there is hell, and a long word that sounds like *hankydoodledum*, which makes no sense. He had no idea that his godfather's voice could go so low. He feels like crying, he can't say why.

*2*  He is part of the choir in a village school so small there are only two classes, and one large ever-hungry cast-iron stove. It is just before Christmas and he has been chosen to be the king who carries frankincense to the infant Jesus. He wanted to sing the king who bears myrrh, its bitter perfume. He is sulking. The infant Jesus is a girl doll in a straw-lined basket, wearing his christening dress, lent by his mother. There will be real animals, they've been told, on the day, but he's sceptical. When his turn comes to sing, his voice breaks on a deity nigh and his teacher, carrying coal to the stove, says no wonder the fire's gone out.

*3* His aunt is living with them, for reasons that aren't clear. In the hall, at the bottom of the stairs, is an upright piano, and his sister is sitting on the stool beside his aunt, who is fine and dry, and speaks in a different way, more clipped and flat than the rest of them. She is his father's sister and his sister is his sister, which means that they will all grow up. There is no escape. It is all a question of practice and application, his aunt says, and his sister nods, and he understands practice but not application, unless it applies to glue, and belonging to something older and flatter than himself, and as hard to learn.

*4* Out of the blue, his favourite aunt buys a record player for them both, a grey and crimson box with a handle on one side. They each choose an EP, his sister opting for Freddie and the Dreamers, while he picks out the first Rolling Stones EP. He plays it constantly, dancing in front of the mirror, his lips and hips thrust out, pouting hands shaking imaginary maracas. Money, he sings to himself. Give me money. He is driven by need as Mick Jagger is, he can see it already in his eyes, and wrists. He is eleven years old and dancing. He dances for his mother and her friends, before the banked-up fire, their amusement a million notes away.

5   Normally he's in bed by half past eight but tonight is a special night and he stays up until ten because the whole world is watching. He is one of four hundred million, although he doesn't know this. What he knows is that there, in the global studio, someone is keeping his place warm for him. By the time they have finished singing he knows the words, which are as easy to remember as words from a nursery rhyme, and he sings them to himself. He lies in bed. Love is all you need, he sings. The next day, in the back row of a school bus on its way to the Royal Show, he sings the entire song, note-perfect.

6   He is watching Eartha Kitt being carried onto the stage of the London Palladium, curled on a leopard-skin chaise longue, borne high on the shoulders of muscular men in loincloths, to purr 'Old Fashioned Millionaire'. He is learning about glamour, and illicit wealth, and desirability, and all of it is a secret to everyone else, his secret. He is learning about the audacity of rhyme, which marries 'in the back' and 'Cadillac' and makes them one. Years later, in a discotheque in Rome, he hears the same voice growl 'Where is my Man', and he realises he's been waiting for her all this time. He's been waiting for the chaise longue and the men. He's been waiting for Malibu. Capri.

7 He is with his closest school-friend and they are becoming cultured by taking whatever the world can offer them. They have seen *Mother Courage* with the school, and *Coriolanus* in the round in modern dress, and raga-jazz fusion. They have hitchhiked a hundred miles to watch Tyrannosaurus Rex and The Nice, and a little less to see Fairport Convention and Soft Machine. Their tastes are broad, and they would like them to be broader. They travel to Manchester for Wagner. Dizzy, exhausted, they perch a hundred feet above a stage where helmeted women have been singing about the twilight of their gods for what feels like hours. At the second interval, they admit it. They have had enough. They dive.

8 So when did music become background? At school, he ordered LPs he'd only read about, dreaming their sleeves like tattoos of nationhood. He sat in their garaged car each Sunday to worship John Peel in holy peace. He wept when David Ackles sang 'Down River'. He studied NME each week, and spent his grant at Andy's Record Stall, and loathed Led Zeppelin and adored Lou Reed and Loudon Wainwright. He measured his ever-changing upside-down heart against Bowie and Diana Ross. He queued in the cold for John Cale, his breath Antarctic cloud. He danced to Kraftwerk in trans-European discos, and George McCrae, and there was no end to it, his boat was rocking, there was no end to the music.

77

9  He's standing in a supermarket in Rome when he hears Joni
Mitchell singing 'Ethiopia' over the tinny speakers. Is that
when it happened? His hands in the freezer, reaching for
calamari or some other luxury item. If music is the food of
love, then canned music is the bolted snack, the hamburger
after the weekend binge, refined carbohydrates, an almost
immediate sense of emptiness. One fart of music and it's
gone, and there is all the noise of the world outside the
store, its traffic and brutal, atonal indifference. Children are
dying, he thinks, his taste for music altered, adulterated, as
the strands of it are woven into the tackier fabric of the
market, from which he'd imagined it immune.

10  Noise greets them as they leave the bus and walk down the
hill towards the square, which is filled with trees and
surrounded by tourist bars. They sit outside the smallest
bar with glasses of soda, the sea at their feet. The sound of
the waves is drowned out by cicadas neither of them can
see. The source of the music is always invisible, he thinks,
and he sips his slowly warming soda and waits for a moment's
silence, an intermission, as though absence were the unin-
vited, welcomed intruder. The sound, he's been told, is
produced by the friction of thigh against abdomen, but he
could easily have been misinformed. They wait for a taxi
to take them somewhere quiet.

14

FEAR

the famished wall

*1*  The bedroom overlooks the garden, which must be where it has come from. He lies on his side, his face towards the moonlight, watching the curtain move in the breeze. He wants the window shut, but his mother and father want it open. There is another bed behind him, but he isn't scared of that. His teddy bear is soft against his chin. The curtain is shifting a little and this might be how it enters the room, passing from outside to inside in tiny particles scattered in the air, confetti, dust, as small as dust until it settles on the chair he dare not look at, and builds into the form of a man, waiting as he is waiting.

*2*  He is standing in front of his mother's wardrobe, staring into the mirror. He shouldn't be in here by himself, but he isn't alone. Behind him is his uncle, but not his real uncle. A man he has never seen before today. The others are downstairs, eating salmon and cucumber sandwiches, but he is upstairs in his parents' bedroom with this man, who is taller than his father and has too much hair, who is standing close behind him and staring into his eyes through the glass, as he is staring into his uncle's eyes so as not to see the hand on his chest, holding him in place, and the other hand with the open razor at his neck.

3  The path leads into the churchyard from the road, high hedges on each side, brambles and yew. It's just wide enough for a bicycle, but bicycles aren't allowed. They walk along it single file. It's cooler than everywhere else, as though a cloud has covered it. There are stories about the path, and about the churchyard, and he believes them, but only when he's alone. He's ten years old, too old to admit he believes in ghosts. The night they get up when their parents are at a party to meet at the mouth of the path they see a white shape moving before them, dragging a chain. They turn and run as it bleats behind them, gurgling like drains.

4  The house is deserted. It's the house they found the empty bottles in, the ones they took to the pub. Downstairs is the green-stained scullery, and the room with the fireplace as large as the wall, which reminds him of a story he's read about a wall that eats the room. There is a bad smell about the place, of dead birds and of something deeper, not dead. They comb the rooms for booty, without success, before going upstairs. The steps are broken in places, but he reaches the top. She's waiting below as he walks into the first room, and then the second, the bad smell stronger all the time. A noise comes from the farthest room. A snuffling.

5   They are stories he reads at night, using a torch beneath the sheets, when the rest of the house is dark. His father has built him a bed above his desk, so he's raised above the room, but none of this matters as he turns the pages of his paperback of horror, each story more awful than the one before. Years will pass and he will still remember the body of the rapist transformed into a monster by a revengeful father and his scalpel, and the gape of the famished wall, and the skittering of the tumour that roams the victim's body at will. There is an eyeball in his palm. The light flickers on, then off. His heart stops.

6   It's during their walking tour of western Scotland. They are holed up in the north-westernmost youth hostel of the British Isles, a gull's spit from Cape Wrath. Among the hostellers a fierce-browed woman is reading a copy of Edgar Allan Poe's collected stories. She has a red pen in her hand and, now and again, with a stifled grunt, she circles something in the text. When she leaves the room to pee, he can't resist. He sneaks a look to see what she's been marking. The word she's ringed, over and over, with a heavy hand, is *blood*. He drops the book, as though scalded. That night, in his bottom bunk, he feels a fumbling at his ankle. He screams.

7  They have been smoking dope all night and someone decides to tell a horror story. He tells them the one about the face like an egg, and then the one about the man banging the boyfriend's head on the car roof as the girl leaves the car and walks towards the lights. Each of them has a tale to tell, as though they have all been waiting for this. One friend talks about a car breaking down outside an unlit house and its driver walking from room to room, each room giving onto the next. Room after room. Door after door. It's a story that ends in its narrator screaming for effect, which is one way of ending a story.

8  His partner can't sleep for sweating. They are staying in a flat that isn't theirs, more beautiful than they deserve; they have nowhere else to go. It is summer and they walk across town each evening, from the Ghetto to the Pantheon, and buy themselves an ice cream, which is all they can afford. They sit on a step and pray for autumn, pray that it will arrive. They have made a mistake and they will have to pay for it. Their house in London had a ghost that kept them awake all night, but they would exchange that ghost for what they have now. The wrung-out sheet, the turning. The word that neither of them is prepared to say.

9   The hospital windows overlook the bay, the castle to the right, a trace of snow still clinging to the southern hills, the island of Capri in the distance. There's a terrace as well, with a table and two yellow chairs, like the ones in the room. Each side of the room has its share of beds, lined up against the walls, a bed, a chair, a bed. The bed beside the window is empty, the weekend case they've brought is open on the chair. He's waiting for his partner to be brought back into the ward. They said the operation would take two hours and he's been gone for more than four. There is no word for what he's feeling.

10   For years he has no fear of age or death. He's a child still, his parents' child, and invulnerable. His Bullworker has been lost in some abandoned home but he's not like Hippolytus, fighting the bull from the sea. He's endless, infinite, a string on which all these shimmering wordy pearls are threaded like breath, like the largest lie a child can ever tell itself, that nothing can ever happen to him. That string that ties him to the world. And then, as though something of little substance has been removed, so silently he barely knows it for what it is, he finds himself with the fearful air in his hand, his parents gone, alone with the chill of it.

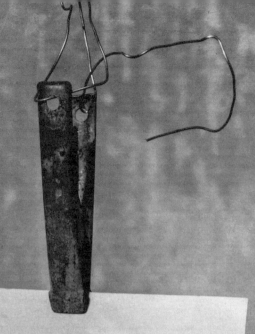

# COLOURS

## 15

OR

*cradling fire*

*1*   For the first years everything is black and white, and has a deckled edge. Each image is as small as his world, in which he is disproportionately large. He is generally the centre of attention. He looks blond, and perhaps he really is. When colours arrive they are greenly bilious or brownish, or the shades of love hearts, pastel, powdery, unreal. These colours fade before long and perhaps what he remembers now is less the colours they were than the colours they became. They are in Wales. He has a short-sleeved shirt, striped blue and black, and his mother is wearing a white dress with a repeated green motif. This is the holiday she dyes her hair purple by mistake.

*2*   To start with colour is a box of paints, round pots of primary colours that make shapes when mixed with water. The shapes are simple, houses, people, dogs, the sun with all its rays. Then the number of colours grows. They come in tubes, and small deep plastic pans and a slim metal box he can slide into his pocket. They come in the way the sky changes at night and moonlight on water, and skin beneath the sun, on card and canvas, and the mutable surface of the world. They align themselves with belief, and political conviction. They form rainbows in the sky, on flags. They are worn in lapels on a twist of ribbon, held by a pin.

*3*  As a boy his favourite colour is red. Some colours you wear as clothes, and some colours you paint your bedroom walls, but neither of these is what he means. Red is the colour that speaks to him, or that he will speak through to others. It is violence, and passion, and blood. He is wondering what it might be like to penetrate these places and the fastest way in is through red. Later, less in love with the notion of violence, aware of the effects of passion, familiar with blood, he changes his mind. His favourite colour is blue. It goes with his eyes, and with the sky. If he has to choose, he would rather fly than burn.

*4*  Eau di nil. Vermilion. Mauve. Is there a time he doesn't know the names of colours too well, with the expertise boys are denied, or pretend to be denied, for their own good? But how can simply *knowing* something be bad, he wonders, and tries out the word brownish for size, and finds that it also fits. It's a question of knowing which word to use, and when. In the meantime, the colours are there, in all their queerness and ambiguity. When each of the pupils at his school is given a strip of earth to grow things in, he doesn't think twice. Among the lettuce and radish of the other boys, he plants a single row of gladioli bulbs.

5  He is lying in bed, imagining what he will do, as an adult, for revenge. He imagines a garden fête, or a wedding reception perhaps, in the garden of the people who have hurt him. They will all be there, standing in smug, self-interested groups, unaware that he's arrived in a chauffeured car, which he will leave in front of the house, the chauffeur inside. No one will recognise him at first, as he walks across the lawn towards the first group. Then someone, a woman, will step back, startled. He will have a copy of his latest book in his hand, his name above the title. He will smile and nod. He will be wearing a canary yellow suit.

6  Each school he goes to has a different coloured uniform. Blue and grey, green and grey, brown and yellow, blue and white. The point of the colours is to mark them out and to make them proud, but he's already marked out, he doesn't know how, and doesn't in any case feel pride. He never asked to go to school. He'll feel pride fifteen years later, and will have his uniform then, a T-shirt and jeans, and a triangle, pink, on his chest, but right now the badges have Latin inscriptions and the colours run when it rains. The uniforms have to be bought from a special shop in the centre, which makes them all equal, except that it doesn't.

7  He arranges his books by colour. All the white spines are
   Picador. One day, he thinks, he will be published by Picador
   and his book will have a white spine, so he is half right.
   There is the block of glossy orange Penguins with black
   and white lettering, and an older block of orange with white
   stripes through the middle. There are green ones, also with
   white stripes, but he isn't so proud of those, and pale grey
   and white ones, which are modern classics, and blue and
   white Pelicans, which are books that have made him think
   rather than dream. And then there are all the other ones,
   of various colours, that don't belong and yet demand their
   place.

8  There is a photograph of him nude on a pebbled beach near
   Bristol, he can't be more than two years old, and his skin
   is so burned by the sun he appears as deepest grey. But no
   one says grey to mean sun-tanned. The more usual word,
   he learns as he grows, is brown. Brown as a nut. He lies
   half-naked in the sun without thought of the harm it might
   be doing, in gardens, on beaches, beside his mother, who
   wears gloves because brown hands are common. In Britain,
   he's brown and proud. In Italy, he's black because what the
   sun does in Italy is turn people black. There's something
   faecal about brown, he suspects, although nobody says this.

**9**  The rooms he has lived in have been mostly white, but his strongest memory of a room from his childhood is the dining room his father built onto their house. Two sides of the room were made of glass, but the rest of the walls were painted orange-tinged red, the colour of Heinz tomato soup. An upholstered wooden bench ran round beneath the sheets of glass and he is climbing onto it, his eyes half-closed, imagining himself at the heart of a round, red fruit, or a cradling fire, the veins in his eyelids darting against the red. He remembers the heat of the room, and his father standing there, holding his arms out for the child to jump towards.

**10**  Six weeks after his mother's death they are sitting in a friend's car and a text arrives to say that Amy Winehouse is dead, and he is taken back five summers to a flat in Paris, on the Left Bank, where they spent a month listening to 'Back to Black', time and time again, and there was a florist's below the flat that belonged to a man of Italian origin, with whom his husband-to-be made friends, and so the flat was filled with roses that had only days to live, their colours both strong and subtle, and they were placed in a copper bowl and painted, time and time again, and there was – there is – no end to their beauty.

DEATH

OR

*a sprig of leaves*

*1* His aunt has lived in bed all his life, at the heart of a double bed she has shared with no one. He sits beside her, feeding her violet-scented cachous until she pushes his hand away, tired. He wants to hug her, and does, her bed jacket soft pink in his face, against his cheek, but one day she is smaller than he is, and he asks her how she feels for the first time. Let's hang up my handkerchiefs to dry, she says, the way we did, and he fetches the wool and stretches a line across the bed. She reaches beneath the pillow for clean handkerchiefs and gives them to him. Peg them out for me, she says.

*2* The day she dies he is sleeping in his bedroom. It is still morning and his mother comes into the room to wake him. She opens the curtains, then sits beside him on the bed and holds his hand in hers. While she talks he watches the aeroplanes he has made from kits and glue as they circle in the draught from the door. Inside the Airfix box, the separate parts are arranged along a central spine of plastic, the whole plane broken up and flattened out, displayed like the rat he saw run over in the road or the machine they use in hospital to measure life, a zigzag and a bottom line. And then his mother leaves him.

*3*  His uncle has the back room. There is a single bed facing the window. He runs into the room and bounces on the bed until his uncle wakes up and makes mountains from his knees for the boy to clamber over. Later, he knocks and hears his uncle cough and spit into a bucket he keeps beside the bed because the lavatory is outside the house and the stairs are steep. Much later, his uncle takes him to the pub and they drink a pint together, and smoke a cigarette. And then he is far away, and his family is falling to bits, and his uncle's skin is as soft as it was as a boy, and he is dying.

*4*  They can see the hill from the top floor, from his aunt's room. It is some miles away, a whale's back of green above acres of low-cost suburban housing, with a prickle of trees along the spine. Except that, now they're here, what looked like a single file of pines, top-tufted like the maritime pines along the consular roads out of Rome, is a series of small groves, planted in lines, leaving space for the odd memorial bench. The oldest deaths are at the centre, more recent ones spiral out like some newly-born galaxy, a swirl of marble slabs placed one against the other, each with its name and date and motto, each with its waffle-topped metal container for flowers.

5  His sister wipes their father's stone clean. They haven't brought flowers because they don't want to think of them dying; they talked with their mother about the virtues of artificial flowers, but decided, in the end, to do without. The stone wiped clean, his sister darts off towards one of the trees, returning with a sprig of leaves. Down one side of the hill is a swathe of stones so tightly laid against one another that the impression they give is of a wide grey road, an uninterrupted sweep of paving slabs. It's hard to see how people can visit their dead without treading on others'. Yet somehow they manage, performing a jittery dance between one stone and the next.

6  His favourite aunt takes him to Dudley Zoo and buys him sausages and double chips. When she comes to visit him in London, fifteen years later, she's shaken by the behaviour of her cousin's husband. Don't tell anyone what he did, she says, and so, even now, he doesn't. He keeps her secret. They smoke dope together the night of Elvis Presley's death; she isn't impressed. Her final room overlooks the road that leads to Lower Green, and then to Upper Green. Her whole geography is here, complete and perfect as the love he feels for her. He tells her this the week before she dies, but she is confused and may not have understood and he will never know.

7 How many people he has met have died without his knowing? He talks to a friend about death, how lucky he has been to have seen so little, to have lived it at second and third remove. How fortunate we are, he says, but his friend disagrees and lists them, writers, poets, artists he has known and loved. All these losses, like cut flowers. You gave me chrysanthemums once, he tells his friend, a bunch so big you could barely hold them, do you remember? Losses like rust-coloured flowers thrown into a stream, to be carried away and slowly borne down beneath the surface, their petals weighted with water as their lives are weighted. I had no idea, he says.

8 His closest friend from school disappears for almost forty years, and then reappears. An email response to a post he has written about a memory of sleeping in a station, of pills, and music, an era of army greatcoats and shoulder-length hair and dreams of San Francisco. A lifetime ago. His friend is now retired, remarried, a house-husband no more than thirty miles from where they both went to school. A little girl. How could all this have happened to us? they say. This time, that past. And so much more ahead of us. They plan to meet. You know where this is going, don't you? Even though they didn't. His oldest friend, the first of them all to die.

*9* On the other side of the cemetery, as they leave for home, are the graves of children, like a special garden set aside for their amusement. The gravestones are decorated as if for a party, with massive paper flowers and dolls that come up to his waist and rain-sodden teddy bears tied on with garden wire. The impression they make is poignant, but also creepy, as though the bereaved one's attempt to recall the innocence, the playfulness, of the child has been subverted into schlock. We are so bad at mourning, he thinks, so clumsy and wordless, but this isn't what he means. He wonders what it must be like to have lost a child and be orphaned in reverse.

*10* He's thinking about what a good age might mean, how duplicitous and evasive the term becomes when applied to people he loves, his mother, his father. A good age is when people you don't know – movie stars, politicians – die. A good age is when you have had enough, but to have had enough is to have slipped past goodness into something darker, the after-ness of good. The coming down. The little death. How clever that seemed when he was young and everyone was still alive, to talk of post-coital *tristesse*. That sadness that gave the pleasure depth. Ripeness is all. *I'm not quite ready yet.* All age is good, he thinks, so long as you are here to grieve it.

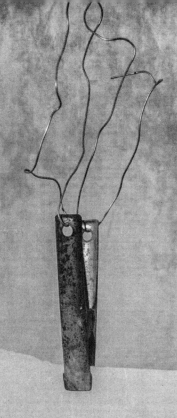

# HOME

17

*some other healing agent*

*1*   His first sense is smell. The smell of apples in an attic. But also sight, because what he can see in the darkness of his head is a floor, uneven, the russet and gold of apples, the whole floor covered with fruit. And then there is touch, as he places his shoe on the edge of this living, scented carpet and feels it move away and then give, with a crunch, beneath his weight. And so hearing is the fourth sense to be woken. He bends down and picks up the ruined apple, its glistening flesh, the bright black of the seeds against the white. He no longer wants to taste it. The fifth sense, he thinks, must be guilt.

*2*   Home is the place he is never alone in, not even in his own room, at night, with the light turned off. Home is the busy-ness of the kitchen, where what's left in the mixing bowl is his, and the oven can burn his hand. Home is the bath-room, where he's not supposed to lock the door, and his mother sings while she bathes him, and his father shaves in his vest, while he sits on the edge of the bath to watch and wonder. Home is the sofa he's lifted off, fast asleep, only to wake up later in his own bed, in his pyjamas, with the man made of clothes on the chair to make sure he's safe.

3　His father is a builder of houses, and a man of quantity. There's a plaque beside the door that says so, with letters and the word Surveyor beside it, which makes him seem to his son like a native scout in a cowboy film, a scout on a piebald horse. But his desk is covered with paper ruled into columns and he works all day and sometimes night to fill them. All the waste paper in the house has columns on its back, columns with numbers and his father's exquisite, illegible copperplate handwriting. So this is how houses are built, the boy thinks, marvelling at the substance of it all, not bricks and mortar at all, but words and numbers.

4　His first home, his second home, his third home. He learns very soon about homes, how they're places that come and go, that shrink and grow to suit some scale, some hidden measure, he can't quite grasp. Sometimes he shares a bedroom with his sister, sometimes he has a room to himself. There are gardens with orchards and greenhouses and lawns, and gardens without, and pantries with marble slabs and pantries beneath the stairs. At one point, fridges enter their lives, and stay. Some houses are more home than others, like some clothes are his and others are handed-down, and never really fit. They belong to someone else, who doesn't like him, and wishes he'd take them off and leave.

5   He has to stop treating his home like a hotel, his mother says, and his first thought is to say that the service in hotels is better, but he holds his tongue and takes some boiled ham from the fridge. Two hours later, he's camped on the roof of his friend's house, in a valley between slate-clad slopes. They've reached the space through a propped-open skylight. They have crisps and lemonade and are prepared to stay there for the rest of their lives, or until someone comes to find them. This is our real home, they tell each other, as the daylight fades and the dark clouds gather, and they're scared to death and would like to be in bed.

6   The family home is where the deepest resentments grow, subtle, relentless as moss, the furring of surfaces organic and gradual, as though life were no longer flesh and blood but bricks and mortar, a suffocation. The collective noun: a suffocation of houses or, rather, of homes. Houses are neutral. Homes are where he's held, transformed into a wailing inmate, convinced of his innocence, but also convinced that his innocence is his guilt, if only they knew. Homes are for the mad and sick, he'll learn, or for something known as rest. He would rather be homeless than be at rest. Meanwhile, his mother stands holding his face, waiting for a change of air, or some other healing agent, to arrive.

*7* His father helps him carry his brand-new trunk into the room. One wall is window, a roof garden outside. The sofa slides out to become a bed, there's a desk, two armchairs. It's his home, and he's waiting for them to leave him so that he can simply be there in it, and be himself. Tomorrow he'll buy an ashtray, and mugs for coffee he'll make for friends he doesn't know, who may already have arrived and be waiting, as he is. His life is in this room and other rooms on the far side of the garden, new friends, first love. He barely notices his parents until they're gone and he sits there, helpless, damp-eyed, wondering what to do.

*8* He leaves a house in the suburbs with a view from the terrace of distant saints and moves into the centre. He has painted doors and ceilings, and a bed made of strips of unvarnished wood like a rack. Naked, he lies beneath the crystal chandelier, now dimmed by a patina of dust, his hands on his stomach. Outside the window he can hear the voices of the young men from the seminary, arguing about which one of them a favourite priest adores the most. The church in the square is called Saint Catherine, its name a corruption of the Latin word for chained. In the house of his own God, he can feel the hard bright pulse of blood.

**9**  The first house they see has no roof and a view of the mountains through a deep hole in the wall. A corner of the attic has been partitioned off to hide a lidless lavatory, elegant as a vase, plumbed into nothing. The attic floor is covered with the husks of larvae and broken tiles. The ceilings of the room below are lined in newspaper whitened with limewash and bemoaning the death of Moro. In one of the rooms an open suitcase made of cardboard contains underwear in various stages of distress. There is a tap, but no water, and a mattress leaning against a wall. They walk around the place, entranced. They make an offer. The house is theirs.

**10**  He moves back into the bedroom that has never really been his, although he has spent at least one weekend a month here for the past five years. It is his parents' house, and then his mother's house, and soon it will be his and his sister's, and then it will belong to a stranger. He sleeps in the room, in the single bed, and then the beds are rearranged and he sleeps alternate nights in the double bed that was once his parents', alternate nights in the single bed beside his mother. He lies there listening to her breathe, waiting for her to speak, or need him, or talk of love. He lies there, sometimes sleeping, always at home.

# WAITING

OR

*from star to star*

*1*  They are standing beneath a bridge to shelter from the rain. They caught the wrong train and now they are waiting for his father to pick them up and take them home. Something is wrong, but he's not sure what. He's too young. Years later, he will see a film in which two people stand beneath a bridge and scream and he will remember this evening, and years after that he will find himself standing beneath a bridge in a town in Portugal with a woman he is supposed to love, and although it isn't raining he will remember this evening once again and the sense of something being wrong, and of him not knowing what to do to help.

*2*  It's been raining for weeks, interspersed with flurries of snow. Just before Christmas, the telegram could arrive at any time. The woman who'll bring it walks miles across fields each day, her bag on her back. She stops at each farm en route, to rest her sopping-wet feet and sip a drop of some seasonal tipple while envelopes are held above steaming kettles. Everyone's waiting for news of someone, or something, not necessarily addressed to them. It's a time of hope, and expectation, and indiscretion. He stands at the door, his mother beside him, waiting to hear if he's been accepted. He's been waiting for years, and he knows it. The postwoman hands him the telegram. You're in, she says.

3 His favourite poet has told him that first love has no impossibilities, but impossibilities are all he sees. He has been waiting since the day he saw him walking across the college garden, his jeans too short, and there is nothing to be done. They have talked about Picabia, and Picabia's palette, and drunk coffee from a series of mugs. They share a love of poetry, and of certain kinds of music. They talk about sex, but words are not enough. He prefers Gary Snyder to Frank O'Hara, which is awful news. Some day he will come through, he thinks, but through what he doesn't know. Everyone thinks they're a couple except them, but maybe one day this will change.

4 The poets take them out for dinner before the reading, the older poet picking up the bill. On the ride back from the restaurant, in the rear of the car, the younger poet's leg is pressed against his. This can't be happening, he thinks, pressing back, but the leg stays where it is. During the reading, he's thinking about the party they'll be holding later in his room. They've bought wine and peanuts and someone will have some grass, he hopes, already drunk from dinner and waiting. At the end of the party, the older poet wishes them both good night. In bed, he listens for the younger poet to finish in the bathroom. He has never been fucked before.

5   He doesn't believe in reincarnation, but if he did he'd be
    waiting for death in order to be reborn. He'd be one of the
    three black girls, the anorexic one with her wild hair, whose
    voice is better than the star's, who stands there and sings
    stage right, her eyes on the crowd, only some of whom will
    notice her. She's always there, she will move from star to
    star, her weight will fluctuate, her hair will fall out and be
    replaced by a series of increasingly extravagant wigs. She
    will have a following who send her letters and teddy bears,
    and offers of marriage, which she'll ignore. She will die in
    Paris, alone, the happiest woman in the world.

6   He is lying in bed, his hand in the hand of the woman on
    the floor beside him. Her cat is dead and she has needs he
    can only deflect. He should have left the country immedi-
    ately after Christmas but he's been threatened by a man
    with a gun and his flat is being used illicitly by football fans
    who can see the stadium from his kitchen balcony. He still
    hasn't learned a word of the language that has purchase
    outside bars or restaurants. Refugees along the coast are
    waiting for homes to be provided, their children wrapped
    in knotted shawls. Everyone is singing fado and eating
    sausages *flambés*. He's been here long enough, he says, but
    she's fast asleep.

7　He applies for jobs in three cities, each one further south than the one before. The first city never replies, the second gets in touch after eighteen months. The third calls him down within weeks and he finds himself in a hotel room near the station, eating from a circuit of inexpensive trattorias. One day, he stumbles upon the set of a film called *Nostalghia*, with the accent on the *ghi*. He tells the technician who halts his way that he's looking for a drinking fountain. The technician says, And I am going north, looking for the source of the chill in my bones. Except that he doesn't. Nobody reads Jack Spicer. He carries on, thirsty, patient, towards the sun.

8　The coffee is not very good, and may come ready sugared. He drinks it slowly, staring out to where he has left his cases, drunkenly heaped against the base of a cast iron lamppost. There are two platforms, the one he uses when he leaves and the one he'll return to. The only way to get from one platform to the other is to cross the track. Sometimes, if he's lucky, he'll shoo away chickens. The train is always late, sometimes by hours, and he will be angry, but deep down he won't care because he has already arrived, without knowing it, and no other place on his holiday will stay with him for as long as this station does.

9   Someday he'll come along. In the meantime, he's doing what all wise shoppers do, he's sampling the goods. He's in the world's heart, a spit from the infant Jesus, wrapped like a wooden faggot in its votive trappings. There's a rock that traitors were tossed off, and he's been tossed off there as well, and a cage where a toothless lion was imprisoned at a later date and he's flirted with the notion of bondage, but slipped away before the history of it all took hold. He's barely had time to meet the needs of one man before another man turns up. It's a dirty job, but someone has to do it. *Someday he'll come along*, the man he loves.

10  He is waiting at the bus stop for his new friend. His new friend is more than a friend already but he's wary about words; he doesn't want to upset him. He called him *amante mio* this morning and was scolded. Lover, he learned, is what you call the *other* person. All he could say was that, no, there will never be another person, because he knows this now. What he wants to say is that *you* are my other person, my other half, but he's afraid he might be rebuked. They'll talk about Plato this evening, he decides. When he sees him get off the bus, he starts to smile, they both do, and neither of them can stop.

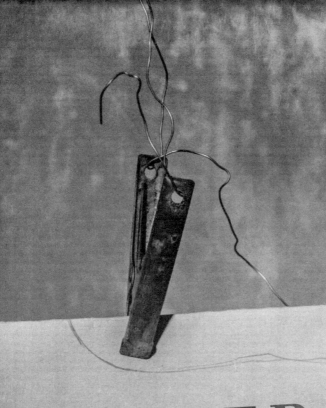

# HUNGER

19

*heavy bones*

*1*   His father would persuade him to eat his supper by making
faces out of the unwanted food. Rows of peas would stand
in for teeth, carrots for eyes, green vegetables – spinach or
cabbage – for a mess of tangled hair. Now eat the nose, his
father would say, and he would shake his head and refuse.
His father was wonderful at making faces from food, so
wonderful he couldn't bear to hurt them. Later, when his
father was nearing death and had no more appetite, his son
spread him marmalade and camembert, as ripe as he could
find, onto wholemeal bread. It's the only thing I fancy, he'd
say. Make me a face, his son would think, and let us eat.

*2*   There was orange juice that tasted boiled, in the bottles
they would later use for lukewarm milk, and bananas on
toast and eggs mashed up with butter and salt inside a cup
for when he was ill. When he had chickenpox, his mother
helped him eat them, sitting beside him on the bed, the
blankets tight across his legs, holding a spoon to his mouth.
On Wednesdays the house was filled with the stench of
boiling tripe that none of them but his mother and his aunt
would touch. When he thinks of music he thinks of tripe,
and his aunt playing scales with the soft, sweet odour of it
on her. The war had finished only fifteen years before.

3 He has a friend who eats sausages raw. He takes the paper
bundle from the fridge, the paper bundle of sausages, and
shakes out the chain of sausages, link by link, before lifting
the last link in the chain. He takes this in his hand and
squeezes the skin until the soft pink mess extrudes. He
bites it off. He rolls it around in his mouth, then sticks out
his tongue with the meat still on it, half-chewed, and lifts
it off to sit in his palm, a wet pale egg. It's your turn now,
he says. He has blond hair, razor cut round the ears. He is
flushed, excited. They stare at each other. They stare at the
meat.

4 They are in a motorway service station, travelling home
after visiting relatives who have given them barely enough
to eat. Plain fare, his father says, and he sees the four of
them flying through the parsimonious air, four scavenging
birds. The restaurant has seating along inverted inlets, with
the customers perched around the coast and the waiter
passing from port to port. They sit in a row, his sister next
to him, his father next to her, his mother at the other end.
His mother orders something with mushrooms, but can't
eat them all. She passes one to his father, who passes it to
his sister, who passes it to him. Opposite them, someone
says, It's a food chain. Humiliation.

5 His mother is trying to lose weight. She eats oddly flavoured Swedish biscuits. She squeezes lemons into water and, wincing, drinks it down. She weighs herself at the chemists' and then at home, her shoes beside the scales. She makes her own clothes. She joins a club and goes to meetings, some of which make her cry. She has a special salad in the fridge, so good they all eat it and she has to make more. She says she has heavy bones. She is beautiful, to look at and to hold, and they tell her this, all of them, but none of it makes any difference. If I lost my appetite, she says, I might as well be dead.

6 They're talking about food, their favourite food, the kind of thing they used to eat when they were children, or sick, or fending for themselves. He tells them about tinned spaghetti, how good it can be when you grate extra cheese into it, and no one imagines he's never eaten any other kind, not yet, and they start to laugh, but no, no, he insists, it's fabulous, I'll do it for you. They're kind, or cruel, he'll wonder later which it was, and yes, they say, that would be great. And so he buys the cans with their yellow labels, and a lump of cheddar, and heats the gooey mass and grates the cheese. And they eat what he's prepared.

7 Their first night in Milan they leave their rucksacks in the hotel, which is next to a fun fair, and begin to walk. Neither of them has a map, nor much idea of what Milan might be, but they aim away from the station towards what they imagine is the centre. It is Sunday and everywhere is closed, it's impossible to distinguish shops from the shuttered lobbies of flats and offices. It's a city of commerce, of power and wealth. They're hungry, but not hungry enough to venture into one of the restaurants they see, where fur coats hang on clothes racks inside the doors, despite the autumn heat. They head back home, wound in by candyfloss, its sickly-cheap scent.

8 When he asks for vegetables to go with his fish, he's offered rice or a fried egg. It's the revolution, she explains, all the fresh food is being sold to Spain. The meat is tough and the milk chocolate-flavoured. Their friends have no money and watch them eat in even the cheapest of bars and cafés. Except for one, which serves winkles, where each has his pin. He watches the empty shells pile up. They drink green wine from carafes. The only dessert he comes across is called Molotov – spherical, vividly striped, indigestibly sweet. The national dish is a hundred versions of salted cod. He's been hungry since the day he arrived and will be until the day he leaves.

*9* He has already eaten by the time his friend gets home from work, but his friend has some grass and so they smoke together, and then make love, and then it is time to eat. They go to the shared kitchen in their shorts and rifle through cupboards and the farthermost reaches of the communal fridge, their bare shoulders touching in the cold blue light. He wants to make toast but there is no bread. He finds some crackers, some butter, an over-sized jar of Marmite that should have been finished five years before. You'll love it or hate it, he says, as he spreads it on the buttered crackers, and his friend says I'll love it. And he does.

*10* He lives in a country where people talk about one meal while eating another and reminiscing about a third. They come back from cities whose names they can barely pronounce and people ask them how they ate. Was it good? *Si mangia bene?* He can't remember the last time he felt hungry. Hunger's the shibboleth, the marker. You're obsessed by food and hygiene, an English friend announces one evening, because you're one generation from dirt floors and famine, and she's right, but not entirely right, and everyone's upset, but continues to eat. He thinks of a scullery in his grandmother's house, and the pressed earth, and the bottled fruits, each labelled with its year. Such riches shored against their deaths.

# NATURE

## 20

OR

*the purposes of love*

*1*  They are sitting on the banks of a pool, the size of a large room, surrounded by trees. It's winter and the branches of the trees are bare. The surface of the pool is coated by a skin of ice the thickness of a sheet of paper. There is a powdering of snow on the fields around them and the ice itself. They are daring each other to crack the ice by putting their weight on the edge of it when the air shatters over their heads into a thousand singing pieces and some object – possibly a bird, but that isn't their first impression, their first impression is of fear – breaks through the ice to disappear in the waters beneath.

*2*  His mother is standing in the room between the kitchen and the garden where they keep their boots and outdoor clothes. They call it the scullery because of the sink in the corner, where they scrub new potatoes free of their soil. She is standing beside the table in the middle of the room, wearing rubber gloves and an apron. The mincer she uses for meat is screwed onto the table. He's scared of it, scared that his fingers, or her fingers, will be trapped inside and turned into blood and meat. She is pushing something into the mincer, her head turned away. Watch out, he wants to say. She is crying. It's horseradish, she tells him, through her tears.

3 He reads about gods having sexual congress with human beings, and falling in love, and changing their loved ones into whatever comes to hand. A tree, a bird, a gust of wind, a flower. Never a house, he thinks, or a fireguard or a garden fork. Never a boat or a bicycle saddle or a mirror. He wonders what it must be like to be transformed into a bird or a flower, a flower so small it might never be noticed unless someone seeks it out. And the gods do it too, they change themselves into birds and beasts. It's as though the whole of nature were spread out before them, like a sample sheet, for the purposes of love.

4 The hens are kept in cages, in rows, stacked three or four high, with corridors between the rows for them to pass. The eggs they lay roll down to a rack along the edge, to be collected. His father has designed the cages so that each hen has more than twice the usual space, but they don't seem to know this. They make a noise you can hear from the house, until you grow used to it. His father says music would make them lay more, but who can hear music above the noise they make. The eggs are striped with shit and sometimes soft, like pouches. He hates the place. The soft-shelled eggs are the ones they eat themselves.

5    He's known what he wants for as long as he can remember wanting. He is eight when the builders next door catch his eye. He stands, dry-mouthed, behind his bedroom curtains, watching the muscles move beneath their skin, praying for sun. At the zoo, he sees a keeper in green shorts and a singlet and falls in love, there is no other word for it, he can see him still. His childhood is starred by the bodies of boys and men, starred and illuminated. His cousin, thin as a rake, adored. A boy in the village, his shirt tied round his waist as he walks ahead, still there. None of it forced, or learned. All of it natural as breath.

6    His tutor calls him in to talk about his lack of drive. He listens to the man tick off a list of absences, unwritten essays, skipped supervisions, his failure to show at lectures. In a fit of calculated madness, he tells his tutor he has unnatural desires. A friend of his had tried this and marvelled as his tutor locked a framed portrait of wife and child into a drawer and stroked him encouragingly on the thigh. This isn't quite what he wants, but neither does he want to work. His tutor, though, backs off. You must talk to your doctor, he says, his face snapped shut. His doctor's name is Strangeways. He thinks about going, but decides against it.

7   His first Italian garden, poised above a lake, he breathes out. He loves box hedges for what they are and for what they say they are. Gardens as boxes of human ingenuity. The nature of who we are and what we want as we work on that other nature, the one that bends to our will, or lets us think so. Because every garden is a war against nature as well, the more natural the more bitterly fought. A formal garden is the concession that other, perhaps more generous, nature makes to our need for order. It's like a hand that pats our head. A knot, a posy, a wreath, a garland. Nature contracting itself into something we can bear.

8   He's looking at photographs of a holiday taken by friends in the Himalayas. They travel along a road carved into a cliff, and there are lorries and danger and he's gripped by what they must have felt. After that there are mountains, and more mountains, and of course he's *appreciative*, how vast it all is, how white, but at heart he's wearied by such inhuman majesty. He's quickly bored by the sublime, by its indifference, its general blandness. His interest is only quickened when he sees, in the distance, a string of coloured flags, or pennants. They seem to be moving in the wind and that's what the wind is for. Finally. He's been missing the point of it all.

9  His students love what they call *la natura*. They all live in
flats in the suburbs of the capital, most of them drive to
class, one in each car, but that's OK, *la natura* is out there,
waiting beyond the petty, polluting details of their daily
lives, the nature is green and blue and sun-kissed above all,
with amenities to hand, and beautiful, as they are, because
to be beautiful is to be natural and those who aren't are
somehow, well, unnatural, and no one likes that. The other
big thing they adore is *sincerità*, otherwise known as the
failure to see complication. Nature is shit, he wants to tell
them, and cancer, and it's staring you in the face.

10 He is watching the body dissolve, his own body, the body
of those he loves. When his father was dying he watched
the man's blood pulse blue in his hands, his eyes turn from
brown to blue, as though blue were the default to which all
bodies returned, the colour of sky and of water. Does the
world ache, he wonders, as these parts of it ache, with age
and illness. The natural world. Lying in bed beside his
mother he watches a heron settle on the uppermost
branches of a nearby tree, impossibly large, blue sky behind.
It is early morning and she will die within days. Look, he
says, reaching across to take her hand, there's a heron.

# CORRESPONDENCE

21

**OR**

*coterminous with the cat*

*1*    He's holding the kitten up to the mirror, but the kitten is restless and wants to be put down. The kitten can't see itself, but he can see them both, and behind them both his cowboy wallpaper, with all the horses pointing the wrong way. His father chose it to please him, but it doesn't, not really; he would have chosen Red Indians, and tepees, and pipes of peace. At school, he'd rather be a robber than a cop, but that's when he's playing with the boys. The girls' playground is better fun, just as long as no one sees him and tells him to leave. His world is coterminous with the cat's. It's a new word, but it works.

*2*    When the school goes to France he doesn't go because his parents can't afford to send him. He stays at home and reads about men who use their single feet as parasols to protect themselves from the sun and sees how the meaning of the word Parasol is contained within it. Years earlier he'd thought that languages were codes and could be deciphered by a simple transposition of the letters, but that must mean *I* and *je* are playing some game he can't understand, where one letter stands for two. How strange it must be in France, he'd thought, where I is other. He learns the word *Parapluie*. He stands unsheltered in the English rain and wonders where they are.

*3* He'd like a penfriend but can't find anyone he wants to write to. There is the problem of language first of all, and then of knowing what to say. People in other countries must think differently, he supposes, if people think in words. His first real penfriend is someone called Dawn, who goes to boarding school with a girl he knows. She wanted to write to a boy and he's been volunteered. She writes to him about other boys and what she wants them to do to her, and he knows exactly how she feels, and about her first period, and he has no idea. When his mother finds the letter, and tells him he mustn't reply, he's immediately relieved.

*4* The woman he worked with writes to him from her new home in another country, and he writes a letter back the following day, filled with his new life. He tells her he should have been honest with her about himself, and how much easier it is in letters, and here is the proof of it, he thinks. As he writes all sense of her, her face, her voice, is lost in the rush of listening to himself confess. He reads the letter through once, then posts it before he can change his mind. He's exposed, but happy. She could ignore him, but she doesn't. She understands. He reads the letter through once, then twice. He wishes she'd never answered.

5   How much of what we say is heard, he wonders. And by whom? He's been talking about his favourite books and mentions *Wuthering Heights* and the woman he's with says, how lovely. What's lovely? he says. The way you say wuthering, she says, it really ought to rhyme with smother, you just make it sound so northern, she says. But it is, he says, it is northern. And then there's the way you always sound the final 'g', she says, in words like loving. They look at each other, you haven't heard a word of what I've said, he thinks, but she's moved on to talk with someone else in a language she shares, leaving him speechless in his own.

6   He's fascinated by parallel universes, forking paths, the Borges thing, but also event horizons, those places where time is stopped and flattened out like cartoon cats splayed helplessly across the sides of houses, always there, and yet nowhere. It's how the world looks to him at times, as though what's here and what isn't here can simply be swapped around. He's ripe for structuralism when it arrives, in its knowing double-edged way, like palindromes or mirror-writing, to tell him about the way power works, only recognisable after a certain effort and then immediately as familiar as Life. A User's Manual. But if what counts is what isn't here, he wonders, the smear on the surface of the world is what?

7   He knows he should write but there is always some distrac-
    tion. He has a life to create as a foreigner in a foreign land.
    His language is no longer the one in which he lives, but
    contingent, a marketable asset, the stuff of dreams. He talks
    to himself in this new language, walking along the tramlines
    towards the factory, where he will teach a blind girl in an
    office with a view of a thousand parked cars. He's angry,
    sad, he's testing the limits of this person he both is and
    isn't. What's lost might not be ephemeral, but the heart of
    him. He's changed, but no mirror shows it. It's no wonder
    he finds it hard to write. Home.

8   The last thing he wants to do is read about himself. He
    can't understand these people who talk about identification
    with characters, as though books were some sort of police
    line-up in which the culprit, oneself, is concealed among
    the rest, who have nothing to do with this crime, whatever
    else they might have done, and the game is to worm oneself
    out and say, yes, that's who I am. He'd like to know more
    about the rest of the ill-assorted crew, the short one in the
    ragged jacket, the man with the harelip, the girl whose heart
    and head lines form a single furrow across her palm, the
    weeping boy, the woman he will never be, no matter what.

9 I'll tell you when I see you, he writes. But telling and writing are different and what he says when he sees her is not what he wanted to say at all. There's a slippage between the written and the spoken word, a lack of correspondence. He tells her he's sorry, but she doesn't seem to hear. A chimp's DNA is 98 per cent the same as a human being's, he reads, but what if the difference is as great as that between pain and paint, or father and farther, or as small? All we can hear is what we want to hear, is that what all the noise is saying? Of people calling out names as though they counted.

10 The letters are the hardest thing to deal with. They are squeezed into shoeboxes, or chocolate boxes, or have holes punched into their margins to be organised into lever arch files recycled from his father's office. Handwritten letters with lies in them, and half-lies, letters he remembers writing and letters penned by someone else, surely, and given to him to sign, his own deceitful, conniving secretary. Himself, his grudging confidant. Postcards scribbled in foreign bars, their stamps steamed off and saved elsewhere, pictures of flowers and sepia castles like small sawtooth-edged tokens of love. And then there are those that meant everything, the truthful ones, the heartfelt ones, bundled in with the rest, indistinguishable in all ways from the rest.

CINEMA

22

OR

*what the centaur meant*

*1*  Saturday morning cinema with schoolfriends because his sister is still too young. He has just enough money for his ticket and a choc ice, which he eats with care from its striped paper wrapper, afraid the brittle laminate of chocolate will slide from the vanilla heart, fall to the floor, and melt into the carpet beneath his feet. He's less excited than his friends as the faithful dog hurtles over the cliff-edge. He knows there will be a saving ledge or a passing truck of hay. This isn't the world as he sees it. He is cynical for his age. He watches *South Pacific* there with his parents, his first adult film, and falls unexpectedly in love with a sailor.

*2*  His favourite film as a child is *Ben Hur*, which he sees with his aunt in the Odeon in Wolverhampton. She's anxious he might be upset by the chariot race and the mangled body of Ben Hur's friend and rival, whose name he no longer remembers, but he tells her not to worry. He holds her hand. It's only a film, he says, and she's both reassured and startled that a six-year-old should say this. What she doesn't know, what no one will ever know, until now, is that he will close his eyes that night and he will think of the scene of the body, broken by horses, and when he opens his eyes it will still be there.

3  It's the dancing he loves, and the patterns the dancers make. Their legs become petals, then spokes, then lips. They open and close, they rise and fall. The world of the dance is the theatre and it is black and white, and people sing there, but not only there. They sing in houses and streets and bars, and sometimes they are at war, but the singing and dancing continue as though there were no other way to be understood. They sing out their hearts, staring straight into his eyes through the glittering screen. Love is important, and fame, but mostly love, and when there is conflict it is love that wins out. Later, with colour, everything will become more difficult.

4  He's too young for *Psycho* but that doesn't stop him sending up to the box office a taller friend, who buys a single adult ticket, then opens the exit door to let him in. They sit in the front row, just the two of them in a cinema that's almost empty, watching the first performance of the day. He keeps his head down below the level of the seat back. They smoke cigarettes. In the first scene, he marvels at the marble-like gleam of the shirtless man's chest. They both spot Hitchcock pass in front of the car. The stuffed birds are wonderful, but scary. They smoke cigarettes. There is blood in the bath. The money is in the newspaper.

5   Years later, as a student, he sees *O Lucky Man!* There is a scene in a hospital, a long corridor, doctors and nurses, white coats, a sense of research being carried out, the details escape him. His mother wanted to be a doctor, would have liked him to be a doctor, and it is true, it would be wonderful to heal the sick, to assist the dying, but at night he can no longer sleep on his side, his legs curled up, one arm beneath him, because what he sees is himself from above, with the head of a young man, eyes red with weeping, and beneath the sheet, but please don't touch the sheet, the body of a pig.

6   The woman is plump, poor, a cleaner in an office. She lives in a small grey flat, stops in a nearby bar for a glass of something on her way home. She has children, grown-up children, with their own lives to lead. There is a man. They dance. The poetry is in the pity. The man treats her well, she can barely believe it. She never imagined she'd fall in love again, and with someone so beautiful, so strong. She's been afraid so long, she thinks, without even knowing. She is not understood and then she is part of that not under-standing. *Fear Eats the Soul.* He would have been brave, he thinks. He would have known what to do.

7  He had no idea. He'd read the books, after all, he knew whose daughter he was watching. He waited until the last minute before going in. He sat alone, to avoid distraction. He was Brian Roberts, and then he was Sally Bowles, and then he was jumping on a running board and turning to wave and not knowing how to confess his love. Because they're bound to love you, aren't they? Because blue is your colour. Because for every life there is one film that counts, and all the others are makeweights and his film is *Cabaret*. He stands in the street outside the cinema and waits for the storm his heart has become to take him where it will.

8  Outside the Arts Cinema with a cluster of disciples, George Steiner is turning his nose up at the programme, but he isn't put off. Inside the cinema, he sits between friends, wondering how much he will understand. It is his first Italian film, unless Sophia Loren counts in *El Cid*. There is a slightly absurd centaur, who says, *When nature seems natural everything will be over*. Tibetan chanting, some troglodyte dwellings, a beautiful laughing boy whose neck is snapped, whose body is broken into small bowls. All at once, he's lost in a place he knows well but has never dared visit alone. Years later, he watches *Salò* in Milan and understands for the first time what the centaur meant.

9   The only cinema in town had wooden seats the first time they went, and table fans along the stage to keep the first few rows cool in August. Most of the films they show are cartoons, Italian sex comedies of the cheapest sort, but occasionally there's a horror film. He's always had a taste for shock, and schlock. At the second showing, they're alone, the two of them in their favourite seats, where circle meets stalls. They're watching a man transform into a beast in a wolf-infested wood when behind them in the aisle they hear a shuffle of feet that almost coincides with the clip of the creature's hooves. She screams, he holds her hand. *You forgot your change.*

10   It is summer and he is sitting in the Circus Maximus watching *Barry Lyndon* on a screen the size of a Roman palace. The circus is bisected by the vast white wall, but it's only white by day, when the sun plays on it and shows up the scuffs and grime. By night, it's washed with colour. This evening, an Irish drizzle softens the outlines of trees and crofts, and then there is a battlefield and then a gaming house. How small the people are, he thinks, in Kubrick's eyes. How wrong he was. The chariots must have swept past his ear. He'd like his aunt with him now, in this great arena, to tell her it's only a film.

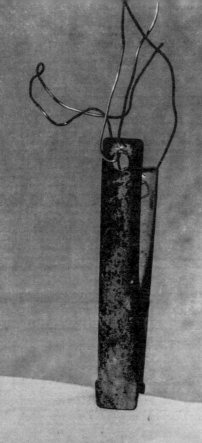

# CELEBRATION

23

*marking time*

*1*    It's his sister's birthday. She's in her bedroom, excited. When the doorbell rings – they're here! – she runs across the landing and down the first flight of stairs, and then the second, past the piano and along the corridor towards the living room. The living room has a glass door and someone has decided it should be closed, but that's no problem, she holds out her arms as she runs, maintaining a constant speed, she's wearing a party dress, but that doesn't slow her down, why should it? It's her birthday dress, they'll be waiting for her beyond the door, she thinks, her hands making contact with the glass, the glass bending slightly, imperceptibly, and then shattering. Blood everywhere. Glass. Tears.

*2*    It is his twentieth birthday and a friend he is secretly in love with arrives in his room and wakes him. He's bearing a bunch of rust-coloured chrysanthemums so big his arms can barely hold them. They plunge the flowers into a bathtub and search the town's charity shops until they find the vase they need, big-bellied, wide-necked. Back in his room, they thrust the chrysanthemums into it just as they come, a rustling mass of leaves and waxy petals, curling like fakir's nails, above the sombre glaze, the same dull rust as the flowers themselves. Decades later, the flowers, which are flowers of death, are themselves long dead. But he still has the vase. He still has the friend.

3   The following year, in a room on the other side of the
college, he comes of age. He doesn't recall the day itself
and most of the evening is lost to him as well, although he
remembers dancing, and surely there must have been food
of some sort, a quiche perhaps, provided by the girlfriend
of the friend whose room they are in. They give him The
Supremes' *Greatest Hits* and he's so delighted they appreciate
his tastes he doesn't see them laughing. He may have mimed
to 'Baby Love' at some point during the evening. The next
thing he knows he's waking up naked in his own bed as a
man and two whole days have passed him by.

4   He goes to visit a friend of his, a poet, who has no money.
It's his friend's birthday. The normal gift would be a book,
some music, but this year he decides the present might as
well be useful as not, and suggests he buy his friend something to wear. They go shopping together in the new mall
in Petty Cury, a place they officially despise. After trying
on various items, a T-shirt, a pullover, his friend chooses
some pale blue jeans he'd never choose himself. He wants
to say No, not those, *the power of money*, but doesn't. He
pays, while his friend waits beside him, holding the bag.
They stand in the street, embarrassed. Happy birthday, he
says.

5  The phone call arrives when he's deciding what to do to celebrate his birthday. It's a young man he met in London that summer, the kind of blond boy you'd expect to carry a catapult in his shorts' back pocket. Hello, he says, I'm your birthday present. I'm waiting for you at the station, and I can't afford the bus. Half an hour later he's in the flat and the celebrations have begun. There are gifts that last a moment, and gifts that keep on giving. And then there are boys who give and take, and think they have a right to everything, and sometimes – like all good things – they're almost lovely, and bright, enough for this to be true.

6  The first of them to celebrate a birthday is the man he loves, and he has no idea what to buy. He wanders from shop to shop. He wants to buy books, and albums, but also something more intimate, a present that will show him how much, and how, he loves him. Another part of him despises presents, their empty gestures. He wants to say, I have given you all I can and have and am, if only that didn't seem as cheap as nothing, if only it couldn't so easily be misconstrued. He will cook for him, and make him happy, and he will know that whatever he does will not be enough, and that will be present enough.

7 His father's ninetieth birthday they're all in Rome. They
have a flat near the English cemetery; they can see the wall
from the windows. They'd planned a stroll around the part
where Keats lies, but his father doesn't want to visit the
cemetery so they take a taxi into town and sit outside a bar
by the Pantheon, and drink cappuccinos. They're marking
time until the evening, and dinner at home. It's what his
father loves, salad and ham and pizza bread and vine tomatoes, and wine. They're laughing together, seated around a
painted table, and everyone is wondering how many more
times this will happen, and nobody says so. When they give
him a wristwatch, he starts to cry.

8 He's fifty and they have organised a party in their house.
People are coming from all over Europe, new friends and
old. The party will last the whole weekend so that nobody
feels their journey has been wasted. Red and white wine
arrive in fifty-litre demijohns, sliced meats on silver-plated
salvers they carry across the town in giggling procession.
He siphons the wine into jugs, and bottles. There are lasa-
gnes and salads and drumsticks, but he barely eats. He talks
to everyone and to no one. He has never received such
presents. He's moved to tears by the cake, and the laughter,
and the love. It takes him a month to gather the final glasses
up and wash them clean.

9  The two of them have been together for twenty-five years. They'd planned a civil partnership and a party, but the year has been given over to smaller celebrations at his mother's house. He likes the word *ricorrenza* for these festivities, for birthdays and anniversaries, name days and public holidays, although all it means is return and the fact that so far none of them is dead. They drink to each other's health and to those around them. They'll have completed a year of celebrations before they leave, but they don't know this yet. They have no idea how long they'll be there, nor that the final celebration will be his mother's death, from which there will be no more return.

10  They book a room in the local Travelodge, opposite the football ground, five minutes' walk from the town hall and the statue of the Lady Wulfrun. The first evening they eat in the local Chinese buffet. The next two days they spend researching restaurants, Indian, Mediterranean, Thai, before deciding. They return to the hotel and find a bottle of champagne and are amazed that Travelodge has guessed their plans, until they find the card. The following morning, after the ceremony, they stand beside the statue in their suits and ties, with people they love, and they drink the champagne from plastic glasses as honest men, amused but not only amused, before eating Thai in a restaurant filled with exotic plants.

# BOOKS

*utterly pliant and clinging*

*1*  They are sitting together on a chair, and his head is resting against her cheek. She is holding a book in front of them, her arm is a little dead where the boy has been leaning on it, if anything can be a little dead, and she is reading aloud the words on the page. She turns the page with difficulty; he's curled against her like a leaf against a stone in running water, utterly pliant and clinging. He is part of her as she reads the book, the words so close to his ear there is no interruption between their utterance and his reception, between her lips as they move and his ear as it presses against her skin.

*2*  The book is called *The Land of Far-Beyond*. He has been given it by his local Sunday school as a prize for attendance, his only merit. The book is a hardback. It has a dust wrapper, which is soon lost, and of which he will have no memory. He will remember the buttercup yellow cover beneath, which will soon fade to beige, and the lettering, which he can feel and almost read even now, with his eyes closed. It is his first prize. The book is a morality tale, an allegory, but he doesn't see it like that. He reads each chapter, over and over again, alone in his bedroom, learning the human faces of Dread and Deceit and Strength.

3   He can read anywhere, he discovers. While his father is watching television, or sitting in the back of the car or on a bus. You get lost in your books, his mother tells him, but that's the opposite of what he gets. What he gets is a sense of where he is so exact he can tell you, or anyone else, each detail, the way people dress and speak, the nature of animals, and of their speech. In his most-loved books there is precisely what is lacking elsewhere. I am *found* in my books, is what he wants to say, as the fictional wind elides his hair and the word-made earth is hard and dry and unmoveable beneath his feet.

4   The boy is on the run, because that is what stories are for. When he comes to a mountain and finds a keyhole for his golden key, he slides the key in and a single leaf of mountain falls, to be followed by another, the stone leaves forming a staircase that leads into the heart of the coldness as surely as the leaves of the book, one page followed by another, lead him into the heart of himself. There is a well there, he can't remember now if there's water. He stands beside the boy as someone listens to their fear. What must I do? the boy wants to know. *You must throw yourself in. There is no other way.*

5   His childhood reading is guided by censors. He's eight when *Lady Chatterley's Lover* goes on sale. His best friend's parents hide their copy behind a Harold Robbins novel in their bedroom, the first place the children look, the white-and-orange striped cover so familiar it only makes the transgression worse. They have buttercups but no pubic hair to thread them through. *Casino Royale* is next in their series of illicit pleasures. He imagines adult breasts as white hills, instinctively avoids a certain type of chair. Seven years later, he sees *Last Exit to Brooklyn* in a bookshop in Worcester and sneaks a copy into his bag to read in the car as his father drives, quietly wanking all the way home.

6   It is a large book and someone has spilt whisky on it, which gives some of the pages, when closed, a wrinkled look, like flaking leaves on a chest in fall. On the back of the jacket is a photograph of the author staring up towards the sky from which all seasons come, even in the city where he lives, so much a part of its fabric its name has become attached to his, a city in which mere nature has been subsumed by the words we use for it. It is a large book and he takes it everywhere he goes, from city to city, in search of his own fatal city, which will turn him into a poet.

7   His mother is almost blind by now. Beside her chair is a CD player and she listens to audiobooks each evening. He sits in the chair beside her, watching TV, or reading a newspaper. Sometimes she chuckles and lifts the headphones away from her ears to shake her head in disbelief. The language in some of these books is shocking, she says, it really is. I can't believe people say such things, let alone do them. What are they saying? he asks her, amused. Here, she says, passing him the headphones. Listen to this. He unplugs the headphones and the living room is buffeted by an account of oral sex in a vicarage. They listen together, smiling, staring into space.

8   His love has been tempered by books. But that's not right, if to temper is to shape what's there. Without books, he might never have been there, or anywhere else, nor understood what love means. In his time he has been a gamekeeper and a lady, a young man with a teddy bear and champagne, a convict in a foreign port whose humiliation is what redeems him, a whore, a child. He has given love, often, and received it. He has learned the ropes of love by being beaten, reeling beneath the other's blow, until his shoulders are burned bare on their roughness and he can only say yes, I will read on. I will learn what I am not.

*9* He hasn't read so much in years. He is sitting beside the window at first and then, when his mother's bed is replaced by a hospital bed, in an armchair wedged between the pair of utility wardrobes his parents bought before he was born. He sits in the substance of her life as it ebbs and narrows, the channel finer each day, and he reads while she sleeps, and then tells her what he has read. She loves to hear his voice, and to know that he is reading. I taught you to read, she says. Do you remember? Yes, he says, although he doesn't, his memory of being taught to read is a fiction. Yes, he says, I remember.

*10* Because he is reading through his mother he has no guarantee that what was read yesterday and the day before that and the day before that is what will be read today, although the story is always the same. The act of reading is an unfolding and there's no knowing what might be newly held within each fold. He listens to his mother's words and his eye sees them and this is how the world is made, by the three of them together, the mother, the child and the book. A history that begins in an armchair in a room with sunlight coming through the window, and the scent of his mother's powder in his nostrils, and his eyes half-closed.

# CODA

### OR

*one bright brief beat*

A month after his mother's death he is home again. It is August and the sky is rowdy with migrating birds. Late morning he walks down the stairs into the hall and sees something move behind the leaning frame of a tapestry his mother made years before, of a garden; he'd forgotten he owned it. Reminded, shifting the frame, he finds a swift. He picks the bird up, quite still in his hand, and carries it to the street to place it on a wall. It pauses, then turns to regard him, grateful, head cocked. Goodbye, he says. Goodbye my darling, says the bird. With one bright brief beat of its wings, it lifts into the sky and is gone.

I'd like to thank all those people — family and friends, too many to name — who appear in this book, for everything they have given me over the years. I'd like to thank Isobel Dixon, for her unswerving support and unbending faith in my work, and Sarah Salway, for her encouragement at a crucial stage. I'd like to thank Scott Pack, for taking an enormous risk, Rachel Faulkner, for her sensitive editing, and Vaughan Oliver, for making the book an object of beauty.

And, of course, I'd like to thank Giuseppe.